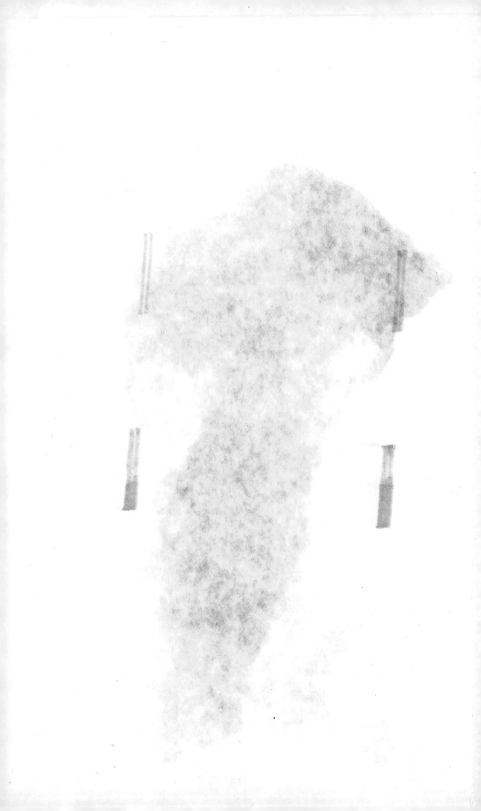

ϕ

NULL

SET

BOOKS BY GEORGE CHAMBERS

Ø NULL SET
and Other Stories
by

George Chambers

FICTION COLLECTIVE  NEW YORK

Some of these stories were first published in the following magazines: *Atlanta, Box #749, Center, Cloud Chamber, Cream City Review, Edgeworks, Epoch, Fiction International, Fogdogs, Northeast, Northwest Review, Sou'wester, Vagabond* and *Wisconsin Review.*

"The Cake" was also published in *The Iowa Book of Short Fictions.* *"TH/ING" was published in Statements.*

This publication is in part made possible with support from the National Endowment for the Arts in Washington, D.C., a Federal agency, the New York State Council on the Arts, Brooklyn College, the Teachers and Writers Collaborative, and the Board for Research and Creative Production, Bradley University.

Michelle Quinones typed the original manuscript.

First Edition
Copyright © 1977 by George Chambers
All rights reserved
Library of Congress Catalog No. 76-47788
ISBN: 0-914590-34-0 (hardcover)
ISBN: 0-914590-35-9 (paperback)
Published by FICTION COLLECTIVE
Distributed by George Braziller, Inc.
        One Park Avenue
        New York, New York 10016

this book is for by to from
my partner editor justifier of
character last wife Patricia too
close for comfort

CONTENTS

JIRAC DISSLEROV

#5

Sonya has agreed to watch television for a week for 50¢ if she writes down what she watched and when. She agreed to give Jirac 25¢ if he also would participate in the survey. He agreed. For a week they watched the television in America. At the bottom of the report there was a space to write in "additional comments." Sonya said she liked the soap messages. Also she asked why people hit each other so much in America. Jirac was weeping, angry weeping. He wrote:
                    "I have not good English. It was an horror experience. I tell you I want to watch people eating bread. I tell you I want to see people at home in the bed, man and woman kissing their bodies, being so very fucking kind to male and female. I want to see the father carve the turkeybird and send plates of food to his dear children down the table. I want to see a person crying because he is lonely for his mother. I want to see lovers making

11

fucking as I hear you call it in this country. Thanks you for my 25¢. I want to see something human." Then there was no more space to write in.

#6

America! I'd like a word with you!
Go to your room!

#7

Jirac decided he didn't need to know why he was doing it, that he didn't need reasons. After all, Sonya never questions herself. She bakes the bread. She paints her face. She screams at the dog. If you asked her why, she would be insulted. He watched her all day Saturday, then he decided he was wrong. Let her wear the dresses! I prefer to be confused!

#30

Jirac notices a man leaning on a pole. His nose is covered with white adhesive tape and cotton. Also, it is bleeding. Also the man is blotting his nose with a white handkerchief. There are several people watching the man trying to stop the bleeding. Also, there is a big dog watching these proceedings, wondering why there are so many people concerned about his pole. "Hmm," thinks Jirac, "this sight makes the picture of my mother come to mind."

#31

Jirac is waiting in line with his friend who is going to Chicago on the bus.

"Goodbye, old friend, I am seeing you off!"

"Goodbye, Jirac. May we meet again!"

"If God permits."

"May he."

Jirac walks beside the bus as it backs out of the stall. He is waving at the windows which are too dirty to see through. But perhaps my friend may be able to see me. Such a dirty bus to carry my beloved friend. I should have brought my sponge.

#48

My job in your country is "soybean research." With my "team" there has been developed a new idea for soybeans. With some other chemicals we made soybean powder. We discovered that this powder has amazing blotter power. How would you say it? Like a diaper? Our idea is this: to mass produce this powder so that farmers may spread it on their fields to hold moisture. If you happened to hear of the drought in southeast Nebraska last summer, you can imagine what the use of that powder might have meant to the corn and wheat crops there.

#49

I use this soy powder in Jack the Cat's litter box at home. He shits in the powder. Periodically Sonya dips his shit into a bucket and tosses it in our toilet. You know, sometimes Sonya looks at me strangely, an odd look. When we were first married she used to say, "And this is my husband, Jirac Disslerov, the Chemist!" Huh.

#51

You know, in my country we expect a woman to be jealous. I mention this because I have met so many women here who are not jealous. By jealousy I mean sex jealousy. In my country if a woman's man fucks another woman. I ask you: How can a good relationship be created that does not have a firm cement underbuilding of jealousy? Perhaps this is the answer to the problem of your high divorce rate, eh? What do you think about that?

#52

Tomorrow is Monday. The mail will come. My mother will send me a postcard of the new shopper center in Ljubljana. In case you don't know, my friend, that's the capitol of Slovenia, on the lovely Sava river.

#53

Stopping by the woods on a snowy afternoon, Jirac stops to tie his shoe, thinking of the rare privilege it is to be able to walk. I need to tell myself how lucky I am. I need to count my blessings. Yesterday Sonya was so angry at me she threw peanut butter on my best blue shirt. I was outraged and delighted. What a woman! With a woman like that I could not look at this snow and think of suicide. No. It makes me think of the sheets on our bed. Which in turn makes me think of sailboats. When I was a kid I used to sail my little boat on the Sava. Oh Mother!

#53

"I'll fix your wagon." This is an expression often heard in
America, although one does not see many broken wagons. It
is a poetry because it does not mean what it says. At work
someone did me an extraordinary favor. To thank this kind
person I said, thinking to be extravagant. "I'll fix your
wagon!" Which, I discovered, is not the way to use the
expression. (Sonya says it means I'll fix your clock.)

#54

"I am an intellectual!" I said, outraged at Sonya. She sews
all our clothing. The shirt she made for me had these bananas
on it. The print was bananas, their skins stripped back
exposing the meat. My place in this society is insecure enough
without wearing bananas to work. Sonya made a fist and
uttered a Slovene curse too ugly for polite ears.

#55

America: beautiful sad woman in soft sweaters moving by
in locked cars, air-conditioned cars. Through the plate glass I
can see their soft heaving bosoms.

#56

Jirac goes into an "Adult Bookstore." Running out,
inflamed, shocked, angry, overwhelmed. He cannot contain
his tears. When he gets home Sonya holds him in the big
chair, rocks him until he is calm enough to eat supper, warm

bread, chicken stew, a glass of good red wine from the old country.

#57

"What kind of gun would you like me to shoot you with?" This question was spoken to my heavenly dove Sonya at the local high school by Mike Gurlacky. He is one ninth grade member of her HANDS ACROSS THE SEA class which she volunteered to teach. The idea of the class is to acquaint young people with other cultures, in this case our beloved homeland Yugoslavia. Mike spoke this question to our Sonya during the question and answer period after her presentation "Folk Dances of Slovenia." Although Sonya is a big woman, her movements are graceful, and the class seemed to appreciate her demonstration. What do you suppose my little pony replied? Do you think she said, "You disgusting little typical violent American"? Or do you think she might have said, "You pimple on your mother's face" (a favorite Slovene curse, by the way)? No, not Sonya. Sonya danced down the aisle to the boy's chair and gave him a kiss, and then pulled him from his chair and hugged him to her soft motherly bosom. Then, at the end of the hour, she presented Mike Gurlacky with a Slovene peasant pot, a tall thin container for spring flowers. Placing the pot in Mike's hand she said, "Class, some day very soon now this Mike will fill this pot full. You remember, you remember what I say. I am never wrong!" And you ask what my wife is like!

#58

Sonya comes from a Greek root which means "wisdom."

Wise Sonya, as in the old Bible story of the wise and foolish virgins. For example, I have been depressed lately. I have morbid thoughts. Last week I was lying on our bed practicing the shape my dead body would take in the coffin. I was telling Sonya I was getting familiar with the room I would die in, the room in which she would sit beside my corpse as its soul flew up to God. I suppose such thoughts come to all men at middleage when they realize their number of happy years on earth is finite. When the body sends information it is bored. And so on. Anyway, in such a mood I arrived home, my heavy thoughts accompanying me. I tossed off my coat and walked to the kitchen where I could smell Sonya's cooking. There sat my white dove naked on a wooden chair which she had placed on the kitchen table. She held a large wind-up clock between her white breasts. The back of the timepiece was removed and Sonya was demonstrating how the gears worked, how the spring released its coiled energy to the little gear, then to the larger gear, and then finally to the hands themselves which tell the time. "Now you fool, you little Jirac," she giggled, "now you pay attention!" Ah, what a delicious meal we had that evening, what a fine time Sonya The Wise and her Fool Jirac Disslerov had visiting together that evening. (Nevertheless, I still have morbid thoughts occasionally.)

#59

This fellow Disslerov has few of the habits most good folk rely on to make their path through this vale easier. Peas, for example. You don't remember it, but your dear Mama taught you to use a fork and ever since, by means of that tool, you have been able to address yourself to the foods on your plate that require that instrument. But this Disslerov, this beefy jerky Jirac. Sonya has served peas and lamb. He is stunned. He looks down at the plate and tools arranged on either side of it with the consternation that General Luftenkampfe must have displayed when he saw the Allied Forces coming ashore on his sector of the Normandy beachhead. What to do? Which weapon to employ against the enemy pea? Peas. Sonya has tricked him again. If she had served mashed potatoes, he could have dumped the peas in the potato dish and used his spoon. The spoon presents fewer problems. (Your dear Mama gave you a spoon first. Which is why the spoon is the symbol of womanhood in literature.) Fork. Picking it up, Jirac considers both ends, rubs the tines across his forehead to cool himself off a bit, to think. He thinks he may tell Sonya he is not that hungry. No, she would guess his lie. She would guess, and that would lessen the necessary respect that all marriages must enjoy. If the man is to have the upper hand. As God said. Well, that's the problem, folks. Why continue? We leave him there amidst the peas. How can this fool Disslerov's problems concern us in a world gone mad, in a world you would choke on if you couldn't forget the starving kids, the bodies dismembered by shell fragments, the millions of our kind who sit down each evening to a bowl of dust?

#60

My friend Moulin is in love with Maria who is married to Dr. Swets the optometrist. It's a sad story. It's like the movies. In fact, Moulin sings a song called "Maria" from a film. In the meantime, Maria doesn't seem to love anyone. She is content to be called "married" as if that were a solution. But she does at least like Moulin's snappy automobile enough to allow Moulin to drive her home. "Slow down," she says, as the car moves out of the parking lot and into the street. She allows herself to be seen by her co-workers but she doesn't look back. Moulin is hungry for some kindness from her, some gesture, a little token of at least appreciation. "Moulin," she says, "I hate your name." Moulin makes subtle gestures like, "Could I eat my sandwich with you at the cafeteria, Maria?" But she always says, angrily, "I'm *married.*" I find the woman distasteful. Except that she has charge of the computer, work which she does efficiently. But distasteful. I mean it is not even a question of her loyalty to Dr. Swets. I think she is incapable of the noble conviction. An ugly person, that Maria Swets. Moulin is a fool. The story is continuing.

#61

Jirac gets a telegram. It says: IT IS YOUR TURN. He remembers her breasts, her liver and onions, the full moon over her shoulder, her bed heavy with bodies, her pot of roses, her mother, her opinions, her bathroom. He remembers enough. His post card to her says: I HAVE ALREADY MARRIED AS MUCH OF YOU AS I CAN ENDURE.

#80

Sometimes I do the dishes and Sonya resents it. She says, "Thank you for doing the dishes." Which I resent. She is a good woman. She is in the back room now weaving. The judge married us at 11 a.m. at the Courthouse. We came back to the apartment where some friends had prepared a wedding lunch for us. Then we went back to work as usual. It is a good marriage, we are partners. You should have seen the look of joy on her face last Tuesday when I told her we were going to the movies. Her smile flashed about the room. That night we had a little fighting and I broke a dish. She was very proud of me. Later she mentioned this event to some friends who had come to eat with us. "A man should break dishes!" she said, her eyes examining mine to see if I got the point.

#81

for Alice C. Clarke

You asked about my wife, whom you have never had the pleasure of meeting. Speaking very strictly, I have never met her either. We confronted one day in a literature class at the State People's University in Ljub, Yugo. The line in question was Prěsern's,

O, Vrba Srečna, draga vas domača

I forget the argument now, but we both remember the heat & struggle & strive to keep alive the flames of controversy which is the solid footing of any marriage. At the wedding reception in the Mayor's office we tossed frosting at each other. Sonya keeps to this day the little peasant dolls which adorned the cake.

Sonya is totally Balkan (née Šubašić) and is therefore quite a large and shapely woman, with tiny hands like white doves which flutter over the stove as she fries the lamb (favorite Slovene dish) for supper. Her flesh is thick and soft. Contrary to the manner of this country, we do not speak of our manners in the bedroom. Suffice it to say, however, that Sonya still has that strange angry look in her eye, the same

look I first saw on the day we had our O, Vrba Srecna battle.
Now, however, she understands her feelings better, so that
when that look, that glint, peeks from her huge black eyes she
carries me off bareback to her stall on Mt. Parnassus.

It is good to say that I miss her when she is not here. She's
not here now, for example. She's back in Yugo. visiting her
aging mother. She sent me some Slovenian pickles yesterday.
It was her sweet way to tell me she was missing me.

She is a strange woman. I have tried for twenty-three years
now to speak to her about the necessity for moral courage,
about the triumph of principles. She resists such high-
mindedness completely. When I start raging about the moral
order she will either leave the room, or leave a (   ), or
she will ask me if I want a Pepsi (her favorite American
beverage).

But she is in a way very high-principled. One evening a man
attempted to rape her as she walked home from the A&P (her
favorite store in America) here in Peoria. The man was very
strong but Sonya was able to overpower him, throw his knife
in the bushes. Then, by twisting his arm, she led him home.
She did not tell me what happened. She fixed strong rosé
wine (from Yugo., very good, spicy) for us and then went to
make food. I passed the time with the man who was I noticed
sweating, nervous. Then we ate, a huge meal. Sonya slapping
the man on the back, making him clean his plate. After, she
asked me to give him, his name was Peter, $10.00 to visit
Aiken Alley which is the spot where one may indulge in the
lusts of the flesh our frame is heir to. I would say that that is
morals in action. You can see how much I admire her, my
little Sonya, my dove, my cake, my little pony, my dear
broom, my bottle, my pot. O, Vrba Srečna, draga vas
domača!

ACCIDENT

ACCIDENT

Something about the only kind of novel possible being pieces of real, of the real; language, experience as it happens? Rather than what? Invention? The imposition of some "order" on the "material"? Today: Get P. to walk downtown. Paper, mail letter to bank in Denver. $ to kids? What to get folks for Christmas? (Let P. decide.) Get her to make a meatloaf for supper, do we have the stuff for it?

Cold, bright, we walk out. Entering the Post Office we meet Z. coming out. He manages his smile to my words, gesture of the left arm. We buy a paper. P. gets a cinnamon roll at the bakery, looks at all the pretty Christmas cookies. Something about the French Canadian women in this town, soft and ?, "creamy"? Ha ha.

On the way back I notice a blue object far ahead on the street which P. cannot see without her glasses. As we close, people are gathering about the object. Some kind of street repair? A police car passes us. Closer, the blue is a delivery van, flipped on its side. I describe what I see to P. as we hurry toward the scene.

Near the intersection, a blue van is flipped on its side. On the same side of the street about fifty yards distant a cream-colored Volkswagen sedan is smashed into an embankment, its door sprung open, the left front side collapsed, traces of blue paint on the hood. On the road pieces of plate glass strewn between the two vehicles.

We stop when we get to a group of people standing on the curb. There is a white-haired man lying in the middle of the street, blood seeping from a crack on his head onto the black tarred pavement. A fat black-haired woman in an apron is bending over the man, talking to him. Looking up, she says to an ambulance driver, "He says his chest hurts." She is adjusting a blanket around him as two men prepare a metal device to lift him into the ambulance. The fat woman I recognize as a secretary who works in the office in the basement of our apartment building. I can see beneath her skirt. Everybody can see the kinds of underwear she is wearing. She is wearing stockings and high-heeled black shoes.

More people and police have arrived. We can hear the sounds of two-way radios from the fire truck, the police cars. A wrecker threads through the vehicles and stops beside the overturned blue delivery truck. On the side of the wrecker are these words, printed in red on a white background: WE MEET BY ACCIDENT. Talk is coming from the two-way radios that the policemen hold in their hands.

Now some kind of priest is bending over the man. He is smiling down to the man who lies composed, expressionless. A bandage has been taped to his skull. It is absorbing the blood. Steel tubes are lying alongside his body. I move P. into the crowd. It is easier to watch the man in the crowd. Standing alone, it did not feel right to be watching him, or the priest, or the woman's crotch.

Someone has asked what happened and a young girl is talking as she watches the man lying in the street. He was a pedestrian and was knocked down by the blue van. The people who were in the van and Volkswagen are not injured. There is the smell of gasoline. The faces of children are peering out of the windows of the school building where they are having Saturday Bible instruction.

The man is lifted onto a stretcher with wheels and pushed to the ambulance. It moves away slowly. Where the man was lying we can now see a large pool of thick red blood, made darker by the black of the pavement. More people have arrived. In the street is the busted sack of groceries he was carrying. Scattered about are packs of cigarettes (Camel), a plastic net bag of onions, four cans of beer, a bunch of celery, a TV Guide. From the crowd a woman asks a policeman if he wants a paper bag. He does not answer.

The policemen are taking notes. One is measuring distances between the objects involved: the cars, the body, the curbing. The measurer is a pole about four feet long to which is attached two little wheels. After measuring a distance, the policeman lifts up the pole and reads the meter, which is also attached to the pole, near the wheels.

The children from Bible class have been let out, now that

the man has been removed I think. They all carry large white hard-cover books. The title on the cover reads: JESUS IS MY FRIEND. With the arrival of the children, the mood of the crowd shifts. There is talking, visiting as we say. There is some laughter. The wrecker pulls the blue van upright. A man asks me a question I do not understand, his French accent is too thick. I think he is angry I am unable to answer him.

A man is sweeping the broken pieces of plate glass to the curb. The fireman trains his hose on the pool of blood. The force of the water shoves the man's blood and the contents of his grocery bag into a pile at the curb.

There is a man crouching down, taking pictures.

P. is getting cold, so we walk across the river to our apartment. On the way I say, "Thank God something happened." "Yes," she says. The dogs greet us by jumping up toward our faces.

It's just after 10 a.m., still have to decide the whole day. P. is in the bedroom. She's sitting in her satin rocker watching the river, smoking. I read the newspaper. There is a picture of two men kneeling with a dog in front of three rows of dead animals on display, hanging by their throats it seems. Under the picture are these words:

HOUND SENSE AND STRENGTH

Stricken with distemper, Cricket, six-year-old blue-tick hound shown with Dale Small of Pittsfield, right, and his brother Bruce of Canaan, not only recovered but accounted for a season's catch of 65 raccoons. The dog was stricken last year after treeing 33 raccoons, recovered in time for this fall's hunting, a pleasant homecoming for Bruce who recently was discharged from the U.S. Marine Corps . . . .

I decide to watch football on tv all day, but before that I take a walk. I say goodbye to P. but she does not answer. On the street there is one of those women walking along. I cross the street and walk faster to see her. Pretty enough, her breasts seem large. French, dark, she has that look on her, something like what? Is she walking to work? If so, does she work at that house? Is she one of Giroux's "Ladies of the Evening"?

I take a cold piece of chicken from the refrigerator and turn on the tv. The dogs watch me eating as I watch the game between the Dolphins and the Lions.

P. at her desk. She is writing words on large sheets of paper:

6 Death   C Existence vs. essence
20 VERTICAL SEARCH   15 Dirty hands

About mid-afternoon she comes in and says, "I wonder how that man is . . . I can't stop thinking about it, you know what I bet happened?"

I can hear making meatloaf in the kitchen. When she brings it out she says, "What would happen if the VW didn't have insurance?"

Something about ruins, where did I read that? About how ruins stir the imagination. A piece of something. A building. Tintern Abbey.

Good meatloaf. P. so pretty now she has pierced ears, two posts of gold peek out from her red hair. (Friday. Thick rain that should have been snow, I drove her to Dr. Bolduc who called her a "stubborn redhead" and pierced her left ear twice. The first hole was off-center.)

Tv until bedtime. A record: nine hours straight. Two games, news (Getty kid showed up in south Italy without an ear), Cook's *America,* Archie Bunker, a "Crime Drama," (kept a tally of commercials: 44).

Lights out. We make love. P. falls off, the dog beside her. I lie awake holding the other dog, listening to cars going by, later the faint sounds, sighing, grunting, from our neighbors downstairs. I go off finally, as a body is changing heads: baby, monkey, woman, alligator, griffin, Uncle Theodore . . .

Sunday Morning. I let the dogs out. Coffee & bagel. Read in the NYT that Fromm is not optimistic about America. (If I thought about it, I wouldn't be either.) Bagle?

I go for a walk, looks like more tv football today. You know, if I'm walking along and I see another figure walking toward me on the same side of the street I cross over. If it is unavoidable that we must pass, I get tight inside, almost angry . . . walk by with my head down. (The other day walking home from work I saw a figure far ahead of me & was tight, angry, until we met and passed. A young girl with a pack on her back who was forced to smile. I was too.) On the way back I stop at the spot of yesterday's accident. I gather up some scraps of paper, leaves. I notice a child's red mitten on the grass. When I got home I smoothed out the pieces. These are the words:

Dear Bill,

I didn
4th peria
and wrote you
saw you this mo
20 past 8, I was in
class. I might a
    with m

Shopping
calle me up ara
Sweetheart, I ho
wait to see
Raining tomorr
    you at

mee
I garr
Job in t
for someea
I wai
But

't have anything
d, So I went to
    this le rni

wait to see y
Raining tomorr

get you a late
Gift. I'll stop here.

    paper to
ne on Grove Street. But
edn't start till January
I coul
tmas

with

(Smooth these pieces a fragment of plate glass dropped off.)
Looks like snow.

Three hours silence, sitting in a chair. P, in bedroom posing
questions. Like: Izz you Izz o Izz you ain't ma bay-bee?

That man, that old man lying on the pavement. Cold
chicken. P. I insist she walk out with me. We pass the scene,
looking for clues. We are so grateful, it is something to do.
She finds a piece of mirror, asks if I want it. Buy the Sunday
Times. Home again, home again, for more tv. What else is
there to do? Perhaps the phone will ring?

On the pre-game show the blonde lady psychiatrist(?) attaches these words to football:

> *well it isn't violence uncontrolled, it's very care-fully controlled violence, and so it teaches us that we can have aggression, and that it can be held within bounds and utilized, and it isn't just violence itself, that would not interest us, ah in the same way that we're not interested in ah bullfight for example. It is the aggression, the ah determination, the ah very carefully controlled violence, but above all there's a kind of a rhythm to the game in which there is some very clever plays, some very tricky plays, so that there's emotion and ah then there's timeout, ah and then there's timeout, ah and then there is a good deal of intellectual ability, and ah very special timing and a great deal of skill, and it is that kind of complicated play which makes the interest. it wouldn't be of ah interest at all if it were just sheer violence itself.*

> *very much so, I think that it ah for many men it ah rewakens the pleasure that they had as very young men when they played and they identify with the players, and they feel a feeling of triumph, and also there's always a chance that er, a, it's not a stacked deck, they know that there is a chance that the underdog will come from behind and win, and it's that feeling of triumph as well which is part of the identification.*

> *I think that's just great. We have so few in ah our lives that men are allowed to touch one another without worrying about it ah when we're little we can only be touched by mother and dad and later on you*

can't touch a little boy anywhere except maybe ruffle his hair and ah as he grows up only a lover can touch him so ah in certain areas we allow men an expression of their emotion and we allow them the expression of friendship and some of the pats and hugs ah are real feeling, depth feeling, important feeling ah in other cultures men will walk along hand in hand and there's nothing homosexual nothing wrong about it, ahh and they do allow themselves this feeling it's great that we have someplace where ah men can show emotion.

not at all. Ah, the, there has been a study which indicates that football players tend to be much more sexually oriented, they seem to need sex ah and need to express sex more than non-football players ah perhaps because, the study found, there's a cult of the body and they're much more interested in ah bodily things generally, in keeping themselves healthy and ah in the testing of themselves ah most people work only at ten percent of their ability, but certain men and certain women, will not accept that and they push the limit and they're testing themselves against their own limits not against necessarily against the opposite team.

not at all, I think a lot of aggression comes out on the field, ah Rosy Greer is one of the gentlest men that I know and ah the interesting thing in terms of studies is that the men that are considered the most hostile are the least and vice versa one study found that the most hostile on and off the field ah are the linebackers and that the quarterback is the least hostile on and off the field.

> *ah no, not at all. One thing that is unusual that people don't realize is that the* team *really has to be welded together from a personality point of view football players seem to be very self-contained, very individualistic, they are not* team *men, they have very little need for affiliation ah if they were off the field they would not necessarily be Rotarians or join groups and so it's up to the coach to* make *them into a team and from the personality point of view they would not be.*

Thanks, Blondie, very comforting . . . such a "comforting presence" you are. I watch a game awhile, then switch about, too bored to pay any steady attention. About 4 p.m. a steady snow commenceth! Komm susser snow. Bury us and the dead raccoons and the blood in the streets. (Last week a little girl showed P. her picture. When P. asked what it represented, the little girl: "The Forest flooding with blood.")

P. still in bedroom working it out. I broil a chicken, make salad. We eat as the Denver-Raider game continues. P. joins me with the dogs and we watch the rest of that game, the "Thrillseekers," a piece of "The New Perry Mason," a piece of Alfred Hitchcock talking about his movies, then all of *The Glass Menagerie* with Hepburn, so insistent, overwhelming, too stagey . . . too much.

I take the dogs out into what is now about four inches of lovely deep snow. Lights out, we pass out, dull, uncommunicative, the dogs sleeping beside us.

At midnight I wake in a cold sweat. In the nightmare there was a room full of women, P. among them. It is told that she is drinking vodka which I don't want her to do. I leave. I am hanging onto the back of a truck which P. is driving. Fast around corners, trying to shake me off. I do and I am falling slow motion through the air, terrified, falling toward a net of thin silvery wires which will chop me like an egg slicer.

We awake in the morning, the dogs growling, a hard sleet-rain falling on the snow that now must be six inches. Monday morning again, the relief of that, of even a few things to do.

Back to it again, do it when I get shaky, these statistics: blood pressure, temperature (anal & oral), weight, measurements of neck, chest (normal & expanded), waist, thighs. Then, outside: temperature, and especially, barometric pressure (which I connect to mood).

I walk into town, new boots holding well in the slush & rain & sleet and snow ho ho. Paper (for the accident). Buy a pair of pretty black waterproof "to the zipper" boots for P. and a pair of socks for them. Coming back the sound of a fire siren. She's in her room. I tell her I didn't buy boots. Later, I bring them in to her. She tries them on.

Delaying, I finally read the morning paper, refusing to let my excitement take over. Page by page. On page six I see it, read everything else first, then it:

> Harold C. _____, 76, of_____
> was listed in satisfactory con-
> dition at _____ Hospital Sun-
> day for injuries he received in
> a two-car accident at 9:26 a.m.
> Saturday.
> A _____ Hospital spokes-
> man said _____ suffered lacer-

ations of the scalp, fractured ribs and a possibly fractured finger.

Perry G. _____, 34, of 1_____ Street, operator of the other vehicle involved, sustained an injury to his left shoulder, was x-rayed, examined and discharged, the spokesman said.

Police said a 1963 International truck operated by _____ was traveling east on _____ Street and as it entered the _____ Street intersection. _____'s 1966 Volkswagen collided with it, causing the truck to roll over.

Police said _____ fell out of the Volkswagen. Both vehicles were extensively damaged.

So he was not a pedestrian. Disappointed, wanted more details, a picture. It's going to be a long day.

Still raining. P. still in other room. Cold chicken for lunch. Exactly 6½ ounces. Two 8-ounce glasses of water.

Mid-afternoon, still Monday. Walk out with P. to try the new boots. Stop by Post Office to get a money order for Harold C. _____, to cover what we think the cost of the beer, cigarettes, onions, and celery must have cost: $5.75, and 15¢ for the *TV Guide*.

Home again. P. goes back to her room, the dogs following.

I sit in the big plastic chair, watch the rain coming down, waiting.

NOTE: Denver Brocos, Broncoes?, in defensive huddle *holding hands.*

Mail comes: Card from Dr.＿＿＿＿, the landlord, the purchase of which "represents a contribution to the Associations for Retarded Children," conveying Best Wishes for Christmas and the New Year. Note from ＿＿＿＿ "had a case of clap (＿＿＿＿) last week . . . (No worse than a bad cold, really.)" Card from ＿＿＿＿ and ＿＿＿＿ . On one side a hand-painted bird, a Rufous-Sided Towhee. And a note wondering if they should name the child they expect in May, "Towhee."

Still raining. Sound of P. typing in other room.

I don't think I'm going to be able to stop it.

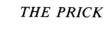

THE PRICK

THE PRICK

There is a woman here now but there wasn't last week.

Last week Betty left with Florin the hairdresser. Betty said Florin was neater. Betty said Florin was orderly.

This woman I met at the Roller Derby Tuesday. She was the one laughing along with the pepsi-cola pop-corn blood so I bumped her on the way out.

She has big bumpers.

"It's yr style," she said.

We went off for a bumper of beer.

"It's yr style," she said and peeled off the comforter on her bed.

When I saw that Betty was leaving I asked, "What about the cat?"

"Fuck the cat," said Betty.

Her dear sweet kitty baby poo-poo catkins. I put the cat on my shoulders and we watched. Florin drove up on the front lawn. He opened the trunk. The landlord came by. He saw the ruts on his lawn.

He stopped his truck and said, "Whyn't you park like a white man?"

Betty walked out with her bag and put it in the trunk. Florin and Betty drove off through the grass. I was relieved but I knew I'd need a woman in about 48 hours. Betty rolled down the window and waved as Florin turned onto the street.

The woman with the bumpers is here now but she won't be here long so I won't give her a name. I'll call her "honey" or "you" if I have to talk to her. I met her at the Roller Derby. I liked her because she was the only one laughing. She had those big bumpers too which I like to see. She took me to her place by the Coney Island Tap.

"I like older men," she said.

"Older men are all business," she said.

I told her my rule about daily medication and she said that would be fine. But that was a week ago and it is clear now that she wants to substitute what she calls "love" for the daily injection. "Love" is a word most women use who would rather not take the daily dose.

It's nothing special, nothing personal. It's simple necessity, daily.

"You dirty nigger," is what honey said this morning.

But I bent her down and laid the pipe anyway. She won't last long. Most don't.

Big bumpers are a problem though. They are valuable just for themselves. If they are firm and if they are slightly irregular. Her bumpers are like that. When a man gets to be my age there is no life left. So a set of jugs like that is like art work to watch, to look at while the bag is filling up again. That's usually about 48 hours for a full load although I top it off every 24.

"You live like a nigger," she said. She was sweeping the kitchen. "All you got is a pension an a prick," she said.

I spit. I don't talk to women. That's what riled Betty.

"Talk to me!" she'd say. "Put yr teeth in an talk to me you jig!" That's the way she'd talk.

Honey wants me to fuck her tits which gives you some idea how unnatural she is.

"Don't you lov 'em, Teeofeel?" That's what the woman says.

Women want to talk and do unnatural things.

I've got a lot on my mind, I can't be bothered with the women except as necessary. Women don't like me much but I never was without one. About a week and they start calling me "nigger" and "hershey bar" and sweeping the kitchen. Then they try not to do their duty.

We are seeing big changes in our world from when I was a young man. It used to be all a man's pride was in his prick. It used to be a woman knew her place, which was bent over.

When a woman wears out get rid of her.

During the First World War I fucked my way through France.

There is hope. My son Harvey calls me now and then.

Harvey says, "Dad, you won't believe where I got my nut this morning."

Harvey is my boy. He sells encyclopedias in Chicago.

"And guess what, Dad? She called me—nigger!"

He's all bat and balls that boy.

It is unmanly to think about dying but when I do I turn my thoughts to Harvey. A man is responsible to the future after all.

The young men of today are confused because there is no moral leadership.

The leaders of old taught by example.

My last day at the station we had a gang-bang and I laid the first section.

There used to be a lot of respect in this country.

Big bumpers. Maybe I could cut them off and hang them on a pole.

I may be one nigger of a prick as they say but I'll tell you they never forget me. They write they call they drop by they stay over they even bring their kids and their husbands and boyfriends. I am glad to see them. After all, history is a fact. And I can tell by how they look at me, I can tell what they are thinking.

I make chili and we talk about the old times and they look hard at the "new one" as they call her.

What I mean to say is that I have the proof.

Harvey is proof.

My health is proof.

My tool is proof.

My mail is proof.

"The proof is in the pudding," as they say.

Today is Tuesday. Big bumpers is talking "love." Big bumpers has not done her duty today.

She said, "Yeah when you got yr health you got just about everthin blackboy, but you ain't gettin' me."

That was early, just at sunrise when I work best.

What I mean to say here is that I intend to preserve the moral integrity of the fibre. The "moral fibre" as it is called.

I'll strap her down if I have to. Why should I let up just because there is no leadership?

About mid-morning. Just before Harvey calls.

"Hey, Dad," he'll ask, "you get yr nut today?"

That's my boy.

I'll slip in my teeth and tell him.

THE RESCUE

THE RESCUE

Once when I was hungry empty for what seemed days at a time, I used to like to read about other folk who had been hungry. Not statistical hunger, not ten million Chinese starving in T'ang T'ao Province (I did mention these dear people once at a family dinner. I said something like you-should-clean-your-plate-because. To which a wise and well-fed young one replied: name two.) but rather, that personal hunger, the hunger of a man in a place and time, a man with shoes and a coat. A man with a name, hungry for, let us say, beans. And so it happened that one winter in my life, a life that if I were to label it I would call happy, I was starving in

47

of all places, Oskaloosa, Iowa. I want here to be quick to say that I bear no malice toward that town, or its generous folk. That is, I don't want it to be thought that those good Oskaloosa and thereabouts neighbors would let a man starve. I suppose they well might, come to think of it, but I have never thought to seek outside help for my condition. My formula was, is simple: no money—no food. The fact that others might have warm and comfortable stomachs and food to share never really occurred to me. Thus, to be hungry was personal, very personal, and I would no more think of mentioning it to my neighbors than I would think of calling attention to my dandruff. Well, to get on, I was starving in Oskaloosa (home, by the way, of the beautiful Justean der Grosse, whom I met much later wearing steel rim glasses and a real leather sarape) that winter, and my hands and heart and mind turned quite naturally to a book about the Donner Party, that group of emigrants to the gold fields of California who spent a long winter in the high passes of the Sierra Nevada starving, some to death, some to madness, and eventually, all to eating their own dead. That was in a time called 1847-1848, but as I read of their tragedy from my own foodlessness, it seemed very much to me as if the Donner Party entire were with me in Oskaloosa, that we were huddled around a pot together, cooking brains.

About hunger I know a great deal by now, because there have been many occasions, or, may I say if you will permit me, many visitations of that personage, quite, to my mind, wrongly depicted as skeleton and shears in the iconography of hunger. I say wrongly because hunger brings a special gift, a gift I shall want to speak of later, in a place which will, I hope, suggest the importance I feel it to have. Well, one thing, one central fact I have come through many times without food to know, is that hungry folk eat more than well-fed folk. That is, well, no need to define it further, definition usually obscuring the ongoing structure of the world as it does (vide here: The researchings of Riemann and Heisenberg). Let the fact serve: that in that winter in Oskaloosa on a day, the LAST DAY, I had in my possession the following edibles, all of which I want to list, to establish a fact, a truth:

Frozen Canadian Swordfish:	4½ oz.
Peanut Butter:	3 tbls. (approx.)
Melba Toast:	1 pk. (8 slices)
Hot Dogs:	2
Margarine:	3 lbs.
Hollywood Bread:	2¼ slices
Cooked Chicken:	½ of a
Diet Soda:	3 cans (12 oz.)

Now what I want to say here is very important, as it will establish the observation made earlier, the one that said, in part, hungry folk eat more. So. As you look, as one looks, at this description of my larder on that day with a full belly, let's say one had just eaten a lunch of salad, onion soup, a sandwich of beef on dark bread, a pickle, and low-calorie preserves, one would probably say that I had enough food, if it were carefully husbanded (or wived, but I had no such helpmeat then, thank God as He only knows) for at least three days, or perhaps even as much as a whole week, with very careful rationing. And, if one's belly were full, that would be quite so, quite reasonable. Or, even if one were just temporarily hungry, let us say it was four-thirty in the afternoon, but that in one's head was the knowledge that at that very moment the goodwife was boiling macaroni for a ham casserole that evening. Even in that condition, I could probably find agreement that a week's food was on hand in my possession on what I am calling the LAST DAY.

And so to the PROOF. On that DAY I ate in one sitting all the items listed above. (Not all the margarine, of course.) The fear, the present, palpable fear of HUNGER drove me that day, as it had so often before, to eat all I had. Quickly, on foot, upright, belching, swordfish undercooked, hot dogs raw, the chicken and peanut butter spooned down together, sloshed with diet soda. To get it, all in, now.

And I know more about hunger too, I know, for example, the freedom one feels when the last spoon of peanut butter is being tongued from the roof of one's mouth. It is what I call the ES IST VOLLBRACT feeling. There is in that feeling peace, certitude, and even, hope. I mean a man does all he can, goes his limit so to speak, and then he, if he is not in debt spiritually, commits himself to the operation of an unknown but no less certain grace with a capital G.

So that, on that DAY, at once fearful and full and free, I sat down at my kitchen table to read of the Donner Party. To starve along with them, and, Deo Volente, to endure.

We were caught in a snow, my God a snow so early and so high, a snow that in October back home on the plains would quickly melt, of fourteen feet by nightfall; a dead snow, a straight down dead thick fat unendurable corpse. And so we thought to make camp, to light fires. (Baylis Williams made a fire and the hot coals of it drilled a twelve-foot hole.) Two more weeks of almost steady snow closed the passes, and thus our minds, to California. We would have, as they say, to make do; to winter it out somehow, here in Truckee. The green grass grew all around, all around. Except that it was white and grew down, and eventually buried the stock.

In my as yet unpublished monograph entitled THE DUTIES OF A PROVIDENTIAL GOD under the chapter heading "Weather Orientations" I remark, to paraphrase, that a PG, mindful of His office and of the dangers inherent in the abuse of power, will seek to control weather operations so that at each point in time and season and place, each geographical sector will experience just enough weather to make fragile human life mindful of its dependency, but not enough to actually kill. This would, I argue, lessen the PG's real power. But, to apply this, considering the plight of the Donner Party (hereafter DP, or the DP) huddled as they are, as we are, under a snow so deep it took them past fear itself, it would seem that the PG is unread in certain important areas. Also, generally speaking, I might say, that in other manifestations of the PG in my own present life, there is certainly no nice discrimination between real and apparent power. We are apt to say God Knows. But, taking thought, we can easily realize that God indeed does not always know. As, witness, the DP under what will be before the winter is out and the rescue has been accomplished some forty feet of snow. That, Mr. PG, is a naked and nude abuse of power. And it is also gross and hankering and mystical.

Well anyway, there I am in my kitchen in the mountains of the Oskaloosa Range of the Sierra Iowa mountains slowly starving to death with the DP, the peanut butter and the chicken and the diet soda making a gas so foul, so intraterrestrial, so entirely diplobotharium latum (L.) so much a presence at all seven orifices as to be further unspeakable. In that condition I rose from my book and, although still quite full of real food and yet still full of the imagination of hunger (which Jung himself mentions in one of his more arcane and later pieces), fell asleep quite noisily on a pile of rugs and newspaper in the hallway. Or, as some may prefer, wrapped in buffalo hide beneath my wagon on the Truckee. My rifle, my trusty dog Dog, et cetera. Anyway, asleep. One can imagine, at this point, the dreams that might arise from this particular psychophysical condition, and I ask that you do imagine them, for they are all germane to my tale.

Everything you think of is mine. My germ. If you get my drift.

Some time before, I mentioned the gifts of hunger, the gifts it brings, gifts of attention, heightened attention incisive, and, too, gifts of imagination. In the ordinary Wordsworthian and altogether common and low world of getting and spending and laying waste of powers, the secular imagination of hunger makes the easy association of hunger and sexuality. Thus, by this common and low standard, the best lovers would be Mysorian Indian males over forty, inhabitant of the B'ing D'ong ghetto on the waterfront in Hong Kong. Witness, so this gross argumentation runs on, the *Kama Sutra,* and the heavy temple, I forget its name, but somewhere in south central Bengal. One appreciates immediately how gross, how pedestrian, such an imagination is. And, we may say, one hardly worth our time. Except to say that it is a truth to which I have been party. I have mentioned the lovely (also "fair" and "true") Justean der Grosse of Oskaloosa. She came upon me once all pure and starved in a midnight clear, and our time together was quite memorable for its duration and versatility. Even her leather sarape and steel rim glasses somehow became factors in that hungry night. But the TRUTH of that time for me was not the prowess of the starveling, which receives much too much maddening attention these days in our fairy life together (so that, as Dali says, the member is vile with gratification), the T-R-U-T-H of it is, or was, that the woman involved in such a circumstance becomes, for the hunger-struck man, an object, entirely a piece of meat, a whale steak, a jelly doughnut, cupcakes. And one's sense is not so much that one is loving, but that one, rather, is eating.

The REAL gifts of hunger, as opposed to those just mentioned (hardly gifts at all, to be sure. Or as W.W., might say, "these hedgerows hardly hedgerows") are of a higher order entirely. The eyes at last come clear. The outer eyes of the body and the inner eye of the soul come to see, to SEE, in detail, the glorious, luminous details. (Surely the good poet himself was starving who could write: I recover my tenderness by long looking (a significant, I think, typographical error occurs in the Robeless edition of said poet's selected work. In that edition the line reads: I recover my tenderness by long cooking)). Jesus I wish I had a ham sandwich now. To see, for example, a plant, a common household plant, to watch it so closely so almost painfully as to see it move toward light, grow, nourish itself, enjoy the air it breathes. This pleasure of God's world. And, with the inner eye, to become that plant, that common household dear little defenseless thing, to become that plant I say, in sympathy absolute. To experience, experientially, such a suchness, a oneness, so that one can say with the great Indian sage: TAT TVAM ASI. This is the true, the HIGHER, gift, of hunger. I really wish you'd give me a pickle.

Late the next day, after a dream much too obscene to record here (it involved, however, a giraffe, an animal I have always detested), I arose from my couch of snows in the Acroceronian mountains, and again commenced to read in the DP. And it is here that I begin to really get at it, as they say. They say, "it comin AT yuh." For, bemidst the terrors of the skull-cracking and arm-chewing starvers I came upon a digression at once so beautiful and so important that it has since become the focus of all my researching. It is, what I call, THE JOTHAM CURTIS STORY. It is, to me, a matter of no small injustice that the main promoters and defenders of the Donner story have so slighted the Jotham Curtis incident. Prof. Steward consigns him to footnotes, Pigney refers to him not at all, and Judge Thornton so confounds and confuses and obscures the story with his adolescent morality as to make it quite worthless. The story is indeed in such disrepair, in such straights and narrows, that in a recent abstract of a monograph in progress at Bob Jones U., the writer questions even the existence in time of the event. Thus, the story of the rescue of Jotham Curtis needs, itself, a rescue. And it should be rescued, for the story has importance, dignity, nobility, honor, sacrifice, all, in short, of those values and virtues the operation of which keep us human and intact and moist and able and ready.

JC wasn't part, directly, of the DP. He had made it over the mountains some years earlier with his wife and meager possessions, and had gone to live as a farmer, he hoped, in the Sacramento Valley. But the world got to him, got too much with him. The sweet security of streets, the ways of man, had so worn his soul, so offended his being, that he thought to remove himself, to go where man trod not and where he, Jotham Curtis, to be henceforthward called KING, might reign in peace and oneness, a very mountain monarch. And so with his ailing wife he had indeed removed himself, had indeed trudged his tiny retinue up and stumble the Salt Creek of Bear Valley until it headed. And just above the valley he had, in September of the year of which we are speaking, set up his own kingdom, where he might no longer be grieved and vexed with the evil deeds of uncircumcised Philistines, or "Flisteens," as he called them. Here he would cease to hear of wrong and oppression; here, in the undisputed possession of his dominions and possessions, he would reign in the vast wilderness forever.*

If I order a bacon, lettuce and tomato sandwich, I usually indicate to the waitress that I require a bit more mayonnaise than is usually to be found on a bacon, lettuce, and tomato sandwich. (Especially, interestingly enough, if it is toasted.)

Now it seems that some members of the DP had indeed

---

*Certain words and phrases, but no clauses, in this paragraph are borrowed from: Jessy Quinn Thornton, *The California Tragedy,* Oakland, California, 1945, p.83.

made it over the high passes before the big snow; and two of those who had made it, one Reed and one McCutcheon, having left wives and children with the main party and imagining their plight, were intent on their rescue, on getting back in there before it was too late with flour and beans and dried beef. And to that end they had mules and horses loaded, and were on their hard and difficult and selfless way up Salt Creek on a thawing February day when they came upon Jotham Curtis wandering in the snow.

Upon seeing these rescuers, Jotham ran at the lead mule, grabbed its neck as if to choke it and, quite unkingly, his lips pressed to the beast's rough and wiry hide, said: "I am saved. I am saved. My deliverance is at hand."

Well of course Reed and McCutcheon thought him starved-mad clean out of his head and mind.

McCutcheon made to lift him to the mule's back, to let him ride on the flour sacked so cosily there, but as he reached to push him up, Jotham bit his wrist, deep. Then there was blood, swearing, a circular pattern of red drippings in the snow.

McCutcheon was about to cuff Jotham with his reredo, but Reed intervened, saying: "It's the hunger on him, leave him be."

Later that day, Jotham hugging the flour sack that was his saddle and screaming occasionally that he was delivered, the men and horses and mules reached the mighty and eternal Kingdom of King Jotham and his Queen.

What the ordinary, well-fed eye saw here in the scrub pine and rock and hard snow above the head of Salt Creek was a sort of animal pen, a pen hastily made of piled logs and branches, and covered with, as the only roof a man could imagine in such a circumstance, a tattered tent. No out-building, no walls and parapets and moats and engines of destruction, no flags and banners and trumpets. Just a crude animal pen with a tent roof.

Jotham crept through the hole into the pen. Reed and McCutcheon followed, after securing the stock.

Inside, squatted before a low fire in which a Dutch oven sat, was the ailing Mrs. Curtis (such has been the neglect of HISTORY in regard to this memorable event, that her first name, a name that might shed no little light on this story, is lost to us). Coughing and weaving back and forth before the fire. So low had they come, so much had been undone, that at this extreme, at this point in a thawing February in extremis, they, the King and Queen, had been reduced, all their stock having either been killed or run off, to butchering their faithful dog, also without name. Said dog was now simmering in the Dutch oven, a heavy cast iron pot with a close fitted lid. Tended by the ailing Queen.

(Dog might not be all that bad. Just the other day I saw a cuddly little bit of meat yapping joyfully in the arms of a young girl. Skinned and eviscerated it would, no doubt, have made a fine, tender, roast perhaps. Or boiled, together with carrots and potatoes. And a few stray cat tails. Eh?)

When Justean Sarape came into my dream that midnight clear, when she actually appeared at the door and knocked her knock, I had been inside a hunger for some three full days. The third day of a well-intentioned and provided hunger is a day of many gifts and many graces. Things are seen on that day which call us, as St. Augustine so often and so justly says somewhere in his autobiography, to the things of this world. And so on that night (did I wake, or sleep?) came to the door the world, a lovely apparition in leather and steelrim glasses. And I knew it was the third day. And I knew that I was blessed.

She said: "Good evening, fellow Oskaloosan. I am from the welcome wagon and I am here to welcome you."

To me she was all amazement and justice, and when I heard

her say that she was the WELCOME DRAGON I knew that I had risen purely above the realm of mere cause and effect, and into the sphere of direct mediate perception.

I said: "Fair, thine Dragon is welcome. May your fires consume away my mortal passages and lead me cleanly to the ham sandwich and the pickle in your basket. May your nostrils of bright fire . . . et cetra."

She then closed the door and sang the dragon tune, that old tradition among welcoming dragons: when it's picnic time in the meadow.

I mention this old picnic, this old memory of a THIRD DAY, because it demonstrates another of the gifts of true starvation. And also, it establishes the fact that to every hunger there is a rhythm, a predictable and on the whole quite orderly rhythm. So much so that given the exact circumstances of any particular hunger-time, one could predict the events, both external and internal, on any given day. And we are, are we not, in the business of prediction? I mean what is science after all?

Well beyond a third day, however, had come our King and Queen. They were beyond prediction, boiling as they were their dog in a pot. Reed crept out of the pen to get some flour, and somewhat later they all, the Jothams, Reed and McCutcheon, sat on the beaten dirt floor to eat.

McCutcheon said: "Very good dog."

Reed said: "Unnnn."

And they all ate to surfeit.

Later that evening Jotham gave orders for his removal to more temperate climes. He would go forth first on the best horse, with three mules as packers; then would follow Reed and McCutcheon, with the ailing Queen packed on a travois behind. Rage indeed was his when he was informed that this was in deed and fact not his deliverance, that R and M were bound for the high passes to rescue the DP. Jotham fumed, spoke of the vileness and cupidity of mankind, screamed that he had shared his faithful dog with scoundrels, and, exhausted, fell asleep before the fire, in which the remains of faithful Fido lay simmering still.

Next morning, clouded and threatening, with Jotham still sprawled dead asleep in ashes, R and M again resumed their rescue operation, leaving flour and beef and beans with Mrs. Curtis, and promising to return when the Donners were safe.

That day proved fateful for all concerned. By midday R and M were in snow to their armpits. At the Donner camp on the Truckee old Kesberg was being accused, in his developed partiality for human liver and lights, of killing Tamsen Donner (a girl of some seven years), and of eating those very parts. And Jotham, having at last awakened from his ashes, was abusing his wife in their animal pen back at Bear Valley. That day the Providential God was indeed unread in my monograph.

R and M kept on their fight with the snow to their armpits and getting deeper until mid-afternoon. But when it began to snow down on them from the heavens above, they turned back, arriving back at the animal pen late that same night, "suffering greatly from fatigue, and with feelings of the deepest dejection and despondency."*

The winter evening in Oskaloosa having descended, I left off in my prayerful reading of the Donner ordeal, marked and closed the book, and, rising from the table in a vision of roast beef done rare, ate a generous tablespoon of margarine done rare, with a side order of salt and pepper. That evening is still memorable, for it was then that I had my first real conversation with my favorite plant, the spotted Dieffenbachia. I guess, my guess is, that I'd always felt closest to this particular plant because part of its name contained the name of my hero the great J. S. Bach. I've always defended

*Thornton, op. cit., p.85.

Bach in his practice of not indicating tempo in his scores, and that evening, through the medium of the Dieffenbachia, I communed with him about it. And, may I say, had the pleasure of hearing the GREAT MASTER thank me and compliment me for the justice and the taste of my defense.* I fell asleep that evening secure in the knowledge that Sebastian loved a good pork pie as much as any man.

After resting a bit, McCutcheon commenced to cook in silence. Jotham Curtis, sitting before the fire with his toes in the ashes, began to abuse his rescuers. Were they not base and were they not vile and were they not full representatives of that species so low and crawling called civilized man. Well, they were were were.

M, maddened and remembering his wrist, kept nevertheless his silence and continued cooking. Mrs. Curtis, trying to assuage her husband's temper, said: "They do no wrong, Jotham, they only cook. Mr. Curtis they do no wrong." And she reminded him too that he ought to be grateful for his deliverance. To this Jotham responded by turning from the fire and beating his wife about the head, calling her names so vile they are impossible to repeat.

Roused by this activity, M said (and here I am following Judge Thornton closely): "Harkee, here, you little mister, you little pictur, I'll put YOU in the fire there and broil you to a cracklin."

He also said: "Stop, or I'll tear off your arms and beat you with the bloody ends."

At this Curtis crouched before the log wall of the pen and glowered at the group around the fire.

Curtis: Vile flisteens, murderers, ingrate infidel slavehide, oarmen . . .

*The Landowska-Gould feud, for example, over tempo in *The Goldberg Variations* is nothing but nitpickereling publicity mongering on the part of two huge recording companies, and does no service to the cause of ART at all. At least to the mind and heart of this humble writer. Some hash browns perhaps?

Mrs. Curtis: Stop, Mr. Curtis.

McCutcheon: Reed, ask that starvling, eelskin snapper, and his wife, to eat of our supper.

Reed: Please come, Mr. and Mrs. Curtis, desist from this despondency and join us in this our repast, our breaking of the bread.

Curtis: I, I, I, ca ca ca can nt can't eat. Eat.

McCutcheon: Why, bedamned and thunder, I know better. You are as hungry as a wolf you fool in the woods. Come right up here now and sit by your wife or I'll shake you right out of your trousers you ugly little pictur you.

And they did sit and eat. Jotham crouching low before the fire, shoving the food in greedily, hungrily, eating more than the rest, pulling at the dried jerky with his fangs.

(I beginning to feel somewhat goofy. My studies are in trouble. The pages look like thin sheets of bread with black ants marching in ranks. I'll need, from now on, to be very careful. I wonder if there is food value in paper? I'd boil my shoes, but they full of turpentine. My Mama left me when I was young it seems to me. She went to garden parties she was a lady she played the piano she was very pretty once I saw her with a football in a picture that Royal Chandler took. He lived in the castle next door. Ives lived there too. He was my friend. Although he was never hungry, one day he shot himself and he was dead. His Daddy understood it because that was his Daddy's job. I cried and cried when Ives died. When Ives died I cried and cried. Ives died cried.)

Although I do not know her well, I feel very kindly toward Justean der Grosse. She has proved, after all, that dragons can be trusted, and that St. George may have been somewhat less than virtuous when he did what all the pictures show him doing. It is better to live with a dragon than kill one. There ought to be rules in this world, commandments, laws, regulations, operating procedures, controls, limitations, food for all, food for me, a bit of cottage cheese with chives.

I mention this kindness I feel toward Justean because there is a knocking knocking hateful rapping tapping at mine door at this very moment. It may be Justean der Grosse, it just may be the great and just lady of the Moors, my Mama, with a football full of beans.

> Who there?
>
> Me
>
> Who me?
>
> Justean you fool in the woods
>
> Who?
>
> The wagon lady
>
> Go way
>
> Jimmy lemme in
>
> Jimmy not here
>
> In
>
> No, Jotham's hungry
>
> Jimmy, open this door. I bringeth succor
>
> Doth Jotham King need a sucker? Doth he not need a substance more befitted to His state and His condition and His fundament. Who howleth in the night at mine moat and door and who defieth mine engine of destruction?

(My advice, if you are to cook and serve MULLED CUCUMERS, I mean MULLED CUCUMBERS, is: serve the potatoes hot with butter and onions, a fresh killed whole milk and drink the blood. Also, FOLD in chocolate and sliced bedorkers. Bring all said items to a raging bowl, scream at the little innocent ones, tell her that you love her. SING THIS:

> fo me to rabbitt
> ain't it a shame
> it's yo own fault, baby
> you got yoself to blame

We left King Jotham and Co. eating before the fire. I'm having a bit of mine own troubles now, it being one of the graces and goodnesses of hunger I have spoken about. And so I'm asking Judge Thornton to come in here and carry the tale onward, to complete this rescue while there is still time. I mean, we need all the help we can get, no? St. Francis, that starving bird, said that. I'm going to quote directly now, so listen up, harkee, or I'll rip off yr ears and beat you with the bloody channels and lobes an tympanums:

> *During the night, when . . . Reed and McCutcheon were supposed to be asleep, Curtis commenced bestowing the most abusive epithets upon his wife for having eaten so readily of the supper. She . . . was frightened out of her wits, and replied . . . that he knew very well . . . they had not a mouthful remaining of the old dog.**

Jimmy, please let me in. It is me, Justean der Grosse
What?
Jimmy, let me in
Did you say let me in?
I have a basket, Jimmy. Please
I am the Lord Thy God. BOOM ROOM TOMB DOOM
Jimmy, I'm here to save you, rescue you
Save you rescue you? What helluva recipe that, eh?
Oh, Jimmy, please open the door
Doth a King needeth doors? What hatha King to do with doors? Eh?
Doth thou egg me? Doth thou bacon me on? Ye foul fish and chips.

*Thornton, op, cit., p. 87. Thanks, Judge

Despised soup! BE YE ENTERED! OPEN YE DOORS AND PORTALS!

The dragon, er, I better say it this ( ) way, (the dragon is here now, having entered my domain and domicile and residence and castle, and she's a good mother and she brung a ball of beans and other delights. She cooking now and the while I am awaiting I needs must get at the rescue regain, to get on with it. Listen to what old McCutcheon said:

Reed, Reed! listen to that
Villainous compound of all
That is cowardly, that
Woman-fighter, that thing
. . . Listen, Reed, she's crying.
Shall I get up, and beat him
*To death**

The story gets complex and even Shakespearian here, so I'm going to take the liberty and shore leave and paraphrase a bit. At this point the recipe calls for "emphatic expletives" all round. For example:

"gosh"
"gee whiz"
"fudge"
"Betsy's bridle"
"sonofagun"
"base Wagnerian soprano"

Then Mac takes Curtis by some parts that shall be nameless and heaves him through the tent roof of the animal pen and into a snowbank. Curtis then comes back and says:

*Thornton, op. cit., p. 87.

I have fallen among thieves.

Then day at length comes. It comes fully hooded and low.
It comes threatening. It comes as snow, as cracking summer
thunder, as God Himself's rebuke at such travail and import
and snorting. It comes chanting the Mantra.

Jimmy! Jimmy! Wake up! It's almost ready. How do
you like steak?
Uh? Wha?
Time to eat, Jim. You good little man.
Dreamed I was in the Spanish Army
He he
What! Doth mine ear deceive me? Ith it base laughter
I hereth?
How do you like your meat?
I must kill something before I eat, fair lady. I must kill
Rare, or medium?
I must kill my plant. It hath grieved me much. Did
you know that Kings speak with *v* instead of *u*? I
mean when they say important things? For example: I
trvst yov. Tough, eh?

As I was saying as it was being said, it is now morning at
the animal pen of Jotham Curtis. Since it was clear to Reed
and McCutcheon that they could not at this time effect the
rescue of the Donners, they decided to go back down to their
base camp in the Sacramento Valley, and to wait there for
better weather. And all was made ready, the mules and
horses loaded again, and they started out with the King and
Queen in tow. They made about four miles that day without
incident, and, late in the afternoon, camped for the night. As
Thornton says, that good man, ". . . they encamped at the
foot of the valley"* (I should and ought and shall say here
THAT I agree with the writer who said, in quite another

*Thornton, op cit., p. 88

context, to be sure, but duly applicable here: EVERY
VALLEY SHALL BE EXALTED, OR EV ree/ Vall ee/ sh
hal/ be/ exhaul/ ted. I mean, it makes good sense. And as
Pauline Plumly once said: It's nothing to sneeze at.)
>   Must needs a sacrifice, a sacrificial death, a kill
>   Jimmy?
>   It must needs be that death cometh with life and
>   therefore
>   You want some milk?
>   Must needs kill my conversation piece my plant I hate
>   it
>   Oh, Jim. Don't do that
>   Plant must die . . . a truly dieffenbachian death
>   ((((here one of the people called me is strangling a
>   tiny green plant in a plastic cup. If this is staged, I
>   might say here that an actual plant isn't necessary,
>   I mean I trust that capacity of the audience, that
>   imaginative faculty, to imagine with their imagi-
>   nations, what I have imagined.))))
>   Kill kill he he
>   Jimmy ho ho, put a leaf in the stew
>   He he he he
>   Ho ho ho
>   He he he
>   Eat, sweet Jimmy, sit and eat now.
>   You are trembling, dear man.
>   I am a man, a mouth, a belly, a God.
>   This stew, Jimmy. Then some steak and oysters and a
>   peanut butter
>   Doth not a King pray before he eats? Am I a prince in
>   the morning?
>   Are there not Bliffo about, recording each act?
>   Ho ho
>   Ho God from Whooooom all wholly desires right

66

counsels and just
works proceed, give to Thy servants that Peace
which the world cannot

That night Jotham again began abusing his wife, and although R and M overheard the abuse they did not interdict. In the morning, however, when Jotham took a brand from the fire and began to build his own fire at the edge of the camp, M grabbed his neck and commenced to choke him with these words:

> *You villainous coward! You panderly rascal! You phrygian turk! You knave! You you!**

McCutcheon kicked him all the way back to the main fire saying:

> *Now march right back . . . and sit down by the fire and behave yourself, and don't let me know you to make a judy of yourself any more, or I'll whip you half to death. If it was not for your wife, we would leave you, and trouble ourselves no more with you. But prudence requires us to take you both in together. But you will, I expect, provoke me to give you a most terrible thrashing.***

Good?
Goood
Erp . . .
Ffffft
Pass the byastifsss
Salt?
Unnnnnn

---
*Thornton, op. cit., p. 89.
**Ibid.

Love me?

Ma ma ma ma ma

Shhhhhhhh

ttttttttttt

beep

ttoot

Jimmy?

shhlurp pip

Jimmylove?

Wha?

Jimmy, there's no romance in our life, all we do is lie around

     and

Faaaaaaaaaa   sssput put

The rest of the trip down the valley to the base camp proceeded without incident, as we say. Occasionally Mc-Cutcheon was heard to refer to Curtis as: *That unconfinable baseness** or: *That base gangorian wight***

Thornton concluded his account of the rescue in this way:

> *After getting out of the snow . . . Reed and McCutcheon gave Mrs. Curtis and her husband all the food that remained, and then pushed on* (to their base camp) *where they arrived in the evening* †

Swuppp

Jimmy, let's go out tonight

Orrrrrrrr

Let's go to a movie

Pffffffft

Let's visit people

---

*Ibid., p.89.

**Ibid., p.90.

†Ibid.

Zzzzzzz, uh
Jotham?
Zzzzzzzz
Jothamjimmylove?

THE CAKE

THE CAKE

Annie was crying, her body one tight muscle. She hated it
hated it, the crying hot itching, having to stand away from
them like that, helpless, at the window, stiff, she could not not
not stop.

They had brought in a cake, Pete and Nevada had come in
from next door. The cake boxed in white cardboard. And
Pete had set it on the floor of the vacant apartment shyly,
carefully, as if it were his child his only son.

He don it, said Nevada.

Pete said, hi that, well ha. And stopped for no more words,
his pocked face in a smile, his hand holding his huge baker's
gut.

She had made fun of them so long, ratflour grease and
retarded kids. Annie had giggled. And their perfect slum of a

name. To be named Dingadore, to have as a name as what everyone would call you: Dingadore. Pete and Nevada Dingadore.

White Line, Annie's husband, came in from loading the truck. Waal, he said, waal waal. Ain't that somethin. Annie, you come over here.

Pete said, it ain't much.

They stood, awkward, pieces of furniture, on the bare scrubbed floor.

Waal, waal, we're goin Arizona. Annie?

She moved from the window, across the bare floor, squatted down in front of the cake-box.

Nevada, seeing one of her children eating dirt outside, said, keep yr fuckin mouth offin that.

Pete moved to the window, back again. He smiled, as if to speak.

Let's go, Nevada said.

Waal, waal.

Look, said Annie. I've packed the forks but let's open the box and have some cake anyway. We can break pieces. I'll break some pieces for us.

They stood around the open box now, looking at the cake. It was round, white frosted. In a red frosting scrawl on top

Pete had written: FAREWELL TO OUR NEIGHBORS.

Annie stooped and closed the box, carefully fixing the cardboard fasteners into the side-slits. Then she went outside, toward the almost loaded truck.

JIRAC DISSLEROV   *201-850*

JIRAC DISSLEROV

#201

Dear Boss: I have to stay at home today. My little dog has the flu. He will feel better if I lie on the couch with him and scratch his ears.

Yr Faithful servant, J. Disslerov

#202

You know, Sonya, I keep trying to understand this America we have here. Remember the one we imagined in Ljubljana, flaming torches, gleaming wheat, and indoor plumbing, do you recall? Well, now I think it is a matter of diet. These people are obviously the way they are because they do not use enough olive oil in their salads and in general cooking. That is the problem. Also, they do not as a rule eat garlic, Inestimable troubles result! My regards to M. Krleza.

Your husand, J.

#203

Oh Sonya I wish you were here today! What I have to tell! You know that infection in my left ear? Well, I stopped by a Doctor on the way home from work, one Alfredo Alcojer, a handsome, courtly man, a native of Madrid. I was directed to a small room to wait. On the wall was a photograph of a lovely courtyard in Granada, with playing fountains. Also on the wall to my right a picture of a huge ear showing how the ear works. I was looking at it, casually, when I realized that in the part designated "ear canal" someone had drawn an obscene object! Imagine my shock. Right there in the ear, a (   ), a, well you remember when we were courting what I called my "Modest Moussorgsky"? Imagine that. When Dr. Alcojer came in to test my hearing I couldn't hear a thing! America makes me deaf! And so on. (I cooked some of your beans for supper.)

Your husband of a thousand years, J.

#204

Telegram to Sonya Disslerov, April Square, Ljubljana, Yugo.

TELL STUPICA I HAVE HIS BOOK STOP
IT IS UGLY TELL STUPICA IT IS UGLY
POETRY STOP TOTALLY DEGENERATE
STOP TELL STUPICA I AM TOO OUT-
RAGED TO WRITE HIM MYSELF STOP
TELL HIM STOP

JIRAC

#277

Sonya! Convey my inexpressible rage to that snake Ducic
on his mountainside of pure poetry, under his warm rock of
patronizing opinions! Remind him that fame narrows the
soul! Tell him that! I say he has created a vicious utilitarian
object unworthy of the name literature. Tell him that! I say!
(Tell him in your own way, of course.)

#278

Ah there was a clarity then, an enemy in uniform, leaders
worthy of respect! How many is the night I dream of Josip
Broz in his cave on Vis directing the People's Liberation
Army. For what I ask myself. So that he could sign a trade
agreement with Pepsi-Cola? So that we could watch "Lucy"
and "Bonanza" re-runs on the television? So what, says
Sonya. Drink your Pepsi, she says. Let's go for a walk, she
says.

#279

On his way home from the annual Soybean Research
Convention in Kansas City, Kansas, Jirac Disslerov is at the
ticket counter to check the time of his flight to Peoria. When
it is his turn, the man in the uniform asks Disslerov, "Where
are we flying today?" Hearing this, our Disslerov flies, of
course, into a rage.

#304

Sonya asking the dog Charlie: "What is your goal in life?"

#305

Sonya! Strange events!

1. Waiting in a long line of planes to take off the ground my fellow passengers are asking how many are ahead of us while I am asking how many are behind.

2. From my room at the hotel I try to make a long-distance telephone call. I call the operator and explain my trouble. She is scolding me, she is saying your trouble is you are thinking, don't think, dial!

What do you think? Obviously these events took place in the America, eh? (So I stopped thinking and my call to Prof. Ravi Tikoo went through.)

#306

Sonya says: What is that toy on those men, is that their price toy?
Jirac says: Oh yes, you have said a wise thing.

#307

What Krelic would call "The Official Boredom of the

Middle Class" such as daily television, infidelity, carpeting, recipes, breasts, knives, dope, football.

#308

Another piece of evidence: These American farmers do not love their animals. They say things like, "The barrow is the end product." Who could eat an animal that was not loved and respected, that did not have a lovely name? In Slovenia, even the chickens have names, even the field mice!, even the gnats and horseflies!

#567

Poem of Farewell:

>Friends! Water is sex and death!
>Fish is woman!
>A man needs a son!
>Goodbye!
>Here's my hat!

#569

Disslerov undertakes a definition of woman: they look like men except in two fundamental ways; #1. They wear bags of milk. #2. They do not wear bags between their legs. Beyond these anatomical matters it is clear that there is one distinguishing feature, a matter of location. A woman cannot tell left from right. If you don't believe me, ask Sonya sometime to hand you the one on the left. Watch closely as clouds of confusion dim her otherwise bright eyes.

#570

Dear Honored Friend Z.! Your situation is intolerable! I understand it completely! I need hardly remind you that pride is the shield of honorable men! But how would worms understand that? Your shield shines brightly in fields of wormshit! History, the last arbiter, will vindicate you! In the meantime, vigilance! I stand with you! The ground quakes but we are firm! I embrace you long distance! Patience!
J.

#571

Sonya, wanting to be American, wants a Valentine on Friday or else. A valentine is a greeting card "of a sentimental or satirical nature sent, usually, to the opposite sex on St. Valentine's Day." Hmmm.

#572

Moon Poem to Sonya Disslerov on Saint Valentine's Day
Sonya! My little moon rising
Before dawn to make skoje and eggs!
Ha ha Sonya, little pieces of night light
As you fry the sausages swearing softly!
When I arise you disappear in a fit
Of noisy domesticity, clattering pots and pans.
I fit a piece of your moon into my sunny heart.

I carry it to work at the Northern Regional Research Laboratories here in Peoria, Illinois

#573

Imagine, dear friends, the catastrophic events that might ensue should you discover one day that you love your wife!

#575

Sonya met an officer of the State Police yesterday. She adores men in uniform. (Except my white chemist's lab smock.) Sonya flirted ("letting the bacon fry" as we say in Slovenia) by asking Trooper Tibbs, as he was called, to tell some exciting stories. Was she disappointed? This Trooper said to Sonya that in 17 years of work his gun has never left its holster. This Trooper told my dear Sonya that the only excitement he has is anticipation of the television shows THE ROOKIES and POLICE STORY. Poor dear S. is so disappointed. But, she says, he did make some tricks with his gun for me.

#800

Jirac saw the lady holding the little baby. The lady was sitting on a sofa with a man and a older child. She was speaking into a microphone. She was saying, "We decided to go Vietnahmese." A curious expression, he thought, a peculiar Americanism. The next day at work he asked his fellow-workers to use that expression in other sentences. "To go bananas." "To go Ford." "To go Colonial." "To go western." "To go Jamaican." "To go wall-to-wall." "To go aluminum siding." And so on. The consensus regarding the locution as employed by the lady mentioned above was that it regarded a decision to buy, acquire, get. Here is our new baby! We have completed our family. We have gone Vietnahmese. We have named our new baby. The baby's new name is "Tiffany." Jirac does not wish to consult his dictionary about that word.

#801

Jirac heard the minister on the radio say this, "When you come home from work, what your wife needs to do is unload."

"So, ok, Sonya," he said that very evening, "unload!"

"Un-what?" she said, looking up from the pan of frying lamb scraps.

"Unload!"

Shoving the meat around with the spatula, she said, "Unload!"

#803

Who is to say what will keep a nation strong and free? Well, Disslerov is modest, but he knows enough to say that our leaders must preserve their constitutional right to secrecy and privacy. Who allowed our great President Nixon to publish those records of private conversations? It is intolerable that we the citizens should know that our leader says (   ) or (   ). Intolerable. The moral fibre of our country is built on our constitution which guarantees to us a separation between public and private. I myself on occasion have said to Sonya, "I don't want a (   ) Pepsi-Cola." But to read that an highest official of our nation said likewise! That destroys moral fibre. And faith likewise. I mean these officials take the Hypocratic oath, don't they?

#804

After a profitable day at market, the peasant is feeling good. He enters a wine shop in the city, orders a bottle of red, a glass. After two hours of meditation in the shop the peasant is feeling ready. "I am prepared," he says. He calls for another bottle and commands the waiter to find the letter-writer. (This old peasant understands that public officials are servants, to be treated accordingly.) The letter-writer bows, takes out his note-pad. "I am writing to my Sonya in Peoria America," says Subasic. "First," says Subasic, "read me some beginnings." The letter-writer consults his book of writing etiquette, reads each possibility to the peasant. The peasant nods, says each one with his lips. The letter-writer reads, "Most Highly Revered Honoured Inestimable Lady Madam." "AH!," says Subasic, "read that again!" Several times, Subasic repeats it aloud. "Very satisfactory, I will take this one, I will consider it. Next week we will continue." It is evening now. Subasic is leaving the wine shop. He is moving slowly down the road that leads to his town. He will walk all night, arriving in time to feed his chickens. As he walks he thinks of his lovely daughter Sonya Disslerov, his shining little girl. To keep him company in the dark, Subasic is repeating the beginning he bought from the letter-writer, "Most Highly Revered Honoured Inestimable Lady Madam."

#807

Sonya is sewing a penis sheath for Jirac (who reads Anthropology for pleasure.). "Hmmm," she says, "moving the fabric around on the pressure-plate of the sewing machine, "this is some architectural problem."

#808

Sonya says she wants to talk to me, but after dinner, when I am relaxed. I am ready I say. Her eyes tell me a monumental question is about to be expressed. "Tell me," she asks, "what is your favorite color?"

#848

LETTER TO THE OFFICIALS:
WE ARE SORRY EXTREMELY WE MUST NOT ATTEND YOUR DANCE NEXT SATURDAY NIGHT AT 9 PM. IT IS BECAUSE WE LOVE OUR HOUSE SO MUCH, OUR DOGS TOOKIE AND CHARLIE AND OUR BRAVE CAT JACK. MOREOVER, WE HAVE NOT BEEN SPENDING MUCH TIME WITH OUR BELOVED PLANTS, ESPECIALLY THE NEW BABY EUPHORBIA AND HER COUSIN THE TITTI-FRUIT. ALSO, WE ARE TIRED OF THE OFFICIAL LIFE. ALSO, WE ARE EXHAUSTED BY THE OBLIGA-TORY DEMANDS MADE UPON US BY YOU IN YOUR OFFICIAL CAPACITY AS MY SUPERIORS, SEC-TIONS HEADS, DIVISION HEADS. WE HOPE YOU HAVE A GOOD DANCE WITHOUT US. OUR RE-

GARDS TO ALL THE KIND OFFICIAL LADIES ALSO
IN ATTENDANCE.

> J. DISSLEROV
> SECTION #8
> (also Sonya D.)

#849

Jirac is reading the great American peasant-poet John
Greenleaf Whittier. Admirable lines such as:

> "No step is on the conscious floor!"

and:

> "I wish to go away to school
> I do not wish to be a fool."

Jirac is outraged at the critics
who speak of the peasant-poet Whittier in these terms:

> "a master of gar-
> rulous vapidity"

"he knew how to pile bricks"   "wild adulatory
effusions"
"not able to organize a poem"

Obviously, capitalistic dogs,
gnomes of private ownership, possessors of literature. Jirac
calls a lawyer, makes an appointment. If there is justice, these
critics will eat their words, without sauce.

#850

Troops of women march out of the moon in June with
baby-rattles and spoons. Here they come! The troops of
women in shining armor, spears and boots. Down they march
on moonbeam roads, singing the song of their leader,
SonyaThe-Wise. "Pots and pans, Pots and Pans, get us a

husband, find us a man." Thank God! Here they come! To the walls men! Thank God, the Enemy is upon us! Load!

THE SURVIVOR

THE SURVIVOR

The boy is placed in a morris chair, his legs not reaching the end of the cushion, his hands moving about the bright yellow and orange toy in his lap. The room about him, a large open place, persian rugs, woven wallpaper, a marble fireplace, a cut glass chandelier refracting light from the giant oak log burning on the hearth, a fixity, a certainty. His mother is seated also, before the black concert grand, her long fingers, strong from many years playing, seeming to hunt among the ivory keys, white and black, as she makes a slow, meditative piece by Chopin.

The boy tucks his toy under one arm, looks past the figure of his mother out the water-streaked pane into the green hill beyond the house, the green made more intense by the spring rain, the rain itself felt through the sad music his mother is playing. Occasionally, there is a crack in the hearth as the oak log adjusts itself to its consummation. The boy reaches for a candy from the open box on the table beside him. He crushes in the tops of two pieces before he finds the one he wants, a hard one, hopefully a caramel. He lets the jacket of dark chocolate melt in his mouth. Then, deliberately, he begins to chew.

He is fallen, a dead pony-soldier, into the thick grasses at the crest of the hill behind his house. Tim and Bill, the indians, have wandered off, leaving him defeated, his skin hot and itchy from play in weeds and dirt. He sights various objects down the barrel of his air rifle, a maple, a barn swallow. From his position on the hill he can see over the thick slated roof of his house toward the city, hazed on the horizon.

In the sky he sees huge, widening letters, five letters that spell the name of a cola. He watches the P as it broadens, turns to a cloud, a mist, is gone. He hears an engine, then sees the blunt nose of a dirigible move as a cloud over him, its shadow passing through him. His father has told him of another airship that has recently exploded in another place. He aims toward the gondola beneath the huge balloon, the rifle slowly moving with the ship. Although he knows a BB could not harm, he is afraid to squeeze the trigger. He spreads his body on the grass. Looking up into the blue, he can feel his body, the world, turning ever so slightly on its axis.

The voice of the principal over the public address system has interrupted class. An important victory is announced, "our fighting men," "the enemy forces," "the end of the war now in sight." The teacher, a thin woman dressed in a white sheet to make Latin seem alive, commands the class to rise, stand at attention, salute the flag.

Then she commands the singing of "America the Beautiful." Later on the same day, playing war again in the field behind his house, he has, from his position behind a stone wall, withstood the assault of the enemy, a force superior to his own. During the course of the battle he has received a BB shot low on his forehead, just above the bridge of his nose. Proudly, he shows the wound to the assembled warriors, especially Tim and Bill. He hurries home to show Edith, the maid, at work in the kitchen. Perhaps she will reward him with a root beer. Edith is distressed, pops the copper bb out of his forehead by squeezing on either side of it with her thumbs. He asks her why there is not blood, shouldn't there be blood, don't wounds always bleed?

The family is in the White Mountains, at the summer home. Although the car bears the letter B on a green sticker on the windshield, the father has turned the engine off at the top of every hill and let the car coast almost to a stop before starting the engine again. Once there, they have all agreed to use the car as little as possible. Friends have come over from their home across the valley. They have brought wild strawberries. A mixture of heavy cream and strawberries has been prepared in a can, and now the children are taking turns at the hand-crank of the home ice-cream freezer. He is wonderering if there will be enough for him, since there are so many people there, since ice-cream is his special favorite. Perhaps the older people will not want some. But now they are coming out onto the porch as the cream thickens and an adult is necessary to finish the cranking. Edith is there with bowls, spoons. There is only enough strawberry ice-cream for a few spoonfuls apiece. It seems to him, however, Edith being his special friend, that she has served him slightly more than the rest. Edith is young and pretty and has hugged him many times. He watches her as she goes back into the kitchen. Still scraping in the mixing can she has given him specially, he hears angry voices from the kitchen. The voices of his father, his mother, Edith. Later he is beside his father in the car as it coasts down the hill toward the railroad station in the Notch.

It is very quiet, the engine off, the tires whispering on the tar road. His father hands an envelope to Edith in the rear seat. She opens it, begins to cry. She tears up the piece of paper in the envelope, throws it on the floor, is crying asking what you think I am. And, I won't take it. When the engine is running again, it seems very loud. Afraid to look at his father, or back at Edith, he watches the road coming toward him, past the B sticker on the windshield.

Pat, the gardener, is a magician because he grows teeth. He can take his teeth right out of his mouth and eat food from his hand. The boy has begged Pat to show his friends, but Pat will only show him.

He has gone down under the floor of the barn, into the dim light, the moist air, to watch Pat working the mushroom beds. Pat looks up at him. Pat goes toward the stone wall foundation, unbuttons his trousers to urinate. Pat holds the thick long whitish part in his hand, the yellow water steaming out, loud and strong as a horse. Pat calls him toward him, asks him to touch that part, go ahead he says.

Touch it. He is about to, then notices the white even teeth smiling from Pat's mouth. He backs away, climbs out of the place under the barn-floor. His stomach is throbbing. Thinking he is hungry, he runs toward the house.

He is waiting, next to jump from the high diving board. His brother, Bill, has gone before him, has made a perfect dive, his body cutting into the water easily as a knife. He is stalled, hears go ahead, jump, behind him, below him. Off the board badly, hesitantly, he is in the air, eyes closed. His body hits the water flat, stinging his skin, knocking the air from his lungs. Later that day, although it is early in August and camp is not over, his father's business partner has arrived to take him and his brother Bill back to the city. There is no explanation. They make the trip in silence. Near home, they are met by his father, transfer to his car for the few remaining miles. On the way, the father draws the car to the side of the road, turns to the two boys in back with tears in his eyes, tells them that their mother is dead. Bill begins to cry also. But he doesn't, he watches them, his brother, his father, weeping. He thinks he had better cry also. He tries, but can find no tears.

Black suit, black tie, black shoes. New. In front of the mirror in his room, looking at the undertaker in the mirror. He must be a new man on the job. The mouth in the mirror is eating a chocolate bar neat. He chases it with a palmful of salted peanuts.

Mary is in an open box in the living room. About her there are banks of flowers, roses, carnations, gladioli. Mary is dead. He has been told the custom: to kneel before her and say a prayer. My Mom is dead. There is stuffed tissue where her breasts used to be. Her hands are folded in prayer, a rosary threaded through her fingers. Up her nostrils he can see wads of cotton. The odor of the flowers comes from her body, sickens him. He remembers her fingers playing the piano, comforting him the day his head cracked open. Before rising he says a "Hail Mary." Throughout the afternoon and evening, people in black go in and out of the house. They pray at Mary's body, then they go into the kitchen to eat and drink. By late evening, Mary is all alone in her box, in her favorite room. The people are drinking, in the kitchen, on the back porches. There is soft laughter, much talk. He goes to the kitchen and is enfolded by an aunt, pressed into her huge, powdery breasts. Her nearness, powder, perfumes, the crude smell of whisky about her, is suffocating. He is called a poor little man. He is told how lovely his mother was, how good a person. Since his aunt is crying, he thinks again that he should also. He moves away. He asks his father for his sister, where is Sophy where is she I want her here. His father says that Sophy, being too young, is in another city, that she has been told her mother has gone on a long trip. Going back into the dead room, he stands by the piano, looking across at Mary. From this distance he can just see the tip of her nose, her forehead where it meets the hairline. From the back porches he hears laughter now. He hears the voice of his uncle telling a joke about a priest, a minister, and a rabbi.

Beneath a stand of pine the creek spreads out to form a small marsh of thick vegetation, weeds, skunk cabbage. Nearby, an open field. He is sitting by a tree, feeling his genital through his trousers. Something is happening. There is an increased, confused tightness, then his trousers are wet. It has felt wonderful. He has no idea what it is. He wanders into the marsh, the pungent skunk cabbage smelling beautiful for him at this moment. As he walks he can feel the sticky substance on his thigh.

In the mirror, he faces a mass of pimples, blackheads. By the use of a special soap, it is called "medicated" soap, and a white cream which, the label says, "makes blemishes vanish," he attempts to organize an acceptable face. He has the feeling that he wants to belong, to be well thought of among his classmates, A clear face is, he thinks, a necessary condition of acceptance. As he works on his face, he repeats the word "blemish" which, he discovers, he likes, quite independent of the horror it denotes. He finds that he is laughing.

At the Lenten season, he is waiting turn for his confession to be heard. The statues of the saints are covered with purple cloth. The church is dim this afternoon, the flickering votive candles the only light. At confession he is relatively new.

What he discovers he needs now is a list of acceptable sins, none too bad of course, but enough to make a confession believable. From the list of activities labeled sin, he realizes he has committed only one. Since that is too shameful to announce to his confessor, he invents others. After he has knelt in the confessional and drawn the curtain behind him, after the priest has slid open the portal and blessed him, after he has begun with the formula "Forgive me Father for I have sinned," he will confess that he has taken the Lord's name in vain, which he has not done. Shriven, he goes to the altar to perform his penance, slowly, so that it will seem enough to his friends who have come with him. Outside, a great weight is lifted. He wobbles down the sidewalk with his friends, joking, delirious.

Everyone is gone. His brother and sister are still at school. His parents, his father and step-mother will not return before dinner. Having left a note, the maid has left early. He hunts through the dresser of his step-mother, a young and beautiful woman. Finding one of her bras, he takes it to the bathroom, undresses, fits the bra on his chest, stuffs it with toilet paper. Finding a jar of his step-mother's cold cream, he slathers it on his genital. He sits on the toilet seat, looking out over the city far away on the horizon under a gray haze. He strokes his genital. He coats the inside of a cardboard center of a toilet roll with cold cream and inserts his genital.
Finding the hole too large, he positions himself on the bathmat and completes himself.

His bat connects with the ball. The sound is momentous. He runs the bases triumphantly. As his cleated foot touches home plate he is aware of the shouting, cheering.

Something is wrong. He has awakened in a sweat. During

the night his mother has come to him, she has accused him of an act he cannot remember. He remembers her lying in the coffin, the stuffy breasts of his aunt suffocating him. He remembers the laughter in the warm August night.

He thinks he must love her because they are naked together on a bed, because he is over her, in her. Above the bed is a gold crucifix, gold. As he dresses, she sits on the edge of the bed angry, demanding that he pay extra pesos. He does not understand, since he has paid the man at the barred window, much as one pays for a movie ticket. He walks out through the courtyard and into the plaza. Next door is the oldest cathedral in Mexico City. He must love her. He goes into the park, sits on a bench, reads in his pocket dictionary.

When the ship docks he is sure there will be fighting, that he will be running down the gangplank firing his rifle. But there is a military band on the dock, playing the Marine Corps Hymn. And there are many young oriental women there too, in pretty dresses, smiling, waving.

He is on a troop train, headed north. Machine guns are set up at the windows, on the roof of the car. In the car are Frenchmen, Australians, Turks. There is excited talk about the war, women. The Turks are eager to loot, which, he learns, is part of their salary. He is bargaining for a hat which he likes, but the Aussie will not part with it.

Of a sunny morning his Lieutenant is sitting on a rock, drying out after the damp night in a foxhole. An incoming mortar is heard. He sees the headless body of the Lieutenant tumble off the rock, his hand clutching his shirt.

The tank battalion has moved into position at the tip of the

Inchon peninsula, at the estuary of the Han River. Some-where across the river is the "enemy." Immediately across the river, on a broad plain, are rice fields and the huts of peasant farmers. It is spring and the farmers are in the paddies, thinning out the new green shoots. The gunners in the tanks are preparing for morning practice. Range is estimated. The breach is loaded with a .90mm shell. He asks the commander why they should be firing at the farmers. He is ordered to watch the hits as they drop with his binoculars, report the accuracy of the firing. Through the glasses he sees an old man, dressed in white, walking beside a rice paddy toward the village of straw huts. The cannons begin fire. In the glasses he sees a puff of dust, pieces of white cloth spinning and twirling in the air.

The man is saying that unless he really loves her and wants to marry her, there is another way. The baby, when it comes, can be put up for adoption. Although he knows he doesn't love her, he insists he does and soon they are married. By the time his first child is born he has gained sixty pounds. Although he eats every moment of the day, as much as a box of candy bars before a dinner of five sandwiches and soda, he is hungry. There is a constant leaden emptiness in his stomach. In time, two more children come. They have happened, he has not wanted them.

But he is pleased with them now that they are here. After seven years his wife divorces him and he goes out to find full-time work to meet the support payments the court has ordered. Within four months of the beginning of divorce proceedings he has lost some sixty pounds. He pleads with his wife to take him back.

Through a white, glaring, antiseptic tunnel, he is carrying

his first daughter in his arms, his other daughter is riding on his shoulders. They are laughing, the white tiles are laughing, they are the teeth of his former wife. As he goes up the escalator the daughter in his arms transforms into a chunk of scrap metal, a huge block of pressed metal heavier and heavier in his arms as he struggles to hold it up.

In some deep place there is laughter, joy. Delight forces its way through him. The sun is gleaming on a green bottle of soda on the kitchen table. He is staring at the words NO RETURN printed into the glass. He begins to giggle, then to laugh. Yes, he is feeling a powerful truth, in his blood, his breath. No return.

As he is walking into the wind along the road he hears himself say that he must move so as not to incur the wind's displeasure. He is pleased with the words, the strange rhetoric of them. Laughing, he repeats the words as he walks along.

Beside the bed, a mattress on the floor, is a serrated kitchen bread knife, a coil of rough sisal rope. The woman beside him has asked him to bind her, torture her. He cuts lengths from the rope coil, ties her ankles tight, rolls her over and binds her wrists behind her back. She asks him to wrap rope about her neck and attach it to the rope about her ankles. He obliges her. As she screams in protest, he watches himself as he rapes her. It occurs to him that the man he is watching is enjoying himself.

He has been with his children, outside, making forts of snow, snow angels, a snowball fight. Everyone is deliriously cold, happy. Inside before the fire, they are eating steak with their fingers. He is telling them a story about a huge talking strawberry. The children are giggling, eager to add their own parts to the story. His youngest daughter begins to cry. She does not want to pack, to return to her home in another state. He holds her for a long while, tries to explain why she must go. She is inconsolable, cries herself to sleep.

Approaching forty, he wonders if he will ever grow up.

"Be a man," is what all women say to him eventually.

Along with friends he has been invited to a formal dinner at the home of an important personage. Two colored women are serving. The conversation is muted, polite. Familiar names of famous figures in history, literature, the arts, pass back and forth in the air. The hostess, a handsome woman in her sixties, is ordering the servant women about in a way that suggests she thinks of them as children, slaves. She begins to talk again, her tone supercilious. The guests are obliged to listen. Beside him a famous poet is struggling at a piece of chicken and is eating it with his fingers. The hostess is continuing her story. Holding the leg in one hand he watches himself as he calls out to the hostess, interrupting her. "Oh," he says, "you are such a bullshitter!" The company is suddenly alive with laughter, relief. Now every one is talking excitedly. The host says, "I think I can forgive you."

His old friend is sinking, drowning. He is powerless to save him. He sees that he must drown, and that he must endure the loss. But his powerlessness enrages him. He takes a whiskey bottle from a shelf and consumes it, to stop the thinking at least for the night. Thinking of all the people he has not been able to save, he begins to weep. He is weeping for himself.

He is asleep in the Hollywood Hills when a violent shaking and rumbling tosses him from bed. He thinks it may be a rock slide, he thinks it may be artillery fire, that the war so long expected may have begun. Pictures fall from the walls, the roaring and shaking continue. He is trying to move toward his friends in the other room when he stops, embarrassed by his nakedness. He hears them calling to him. Then it is over. Across the valley he sees a huge shadow-smudged moon sinking behind the mountains. Both he and his friend begin to laugh, joyful. Both want the shaking to continue, to become even more intense. Laughing, they agree that somehow the moon has willed the quaking. After comforting the woman, the friends sit in the car listening to the radio. At first there is a commercial for a tablet which is to be taken when one has eaten "too well." Then, reports of the destruction begin. For the rest of that day he is completely happy.

He is watching his son ride a motorbike through the field. Although he is enjoying the way his son handles himself on the bike, he thinks he ought to make some cautionary, "fatherly" statement. His son gives him a lesson, shows him how to co-ordinate the hand-throttle and the foot-clutch. The bike under him bites out, speeds away. He is unable to shift it into second gear. He stalls it. His son explains the problem, encourages him to take another try.

With the local birds he is angry. He has told the young woman he lives with that unless the birds eat from the feeder he has erected for them, he'll get a BB gun and shoot them.

The woman is reading *Screen Life*. She reads to him about how much an actress loves her new husband. She reads two new weight-reducing plans to him. Then she goes into the kitchen to make his lunch.

He makes a drawing of various objects in his apartment

which he entitles "Industrial Altar." Now he is painting a mural directly on the white walls of his apartment. It will be, when finished, a collage of parts of women, breasts, thighs, hips, all intertwined, with knives and teeth placed at random.

He places the young woman in the box. He saws through her torso, blood dripping from the teeth of the rip-saw. The audience is pleased, cheers go up.

Now that I have eaten, he thinks, I had better wash my bowl.

WILLIAM

WILLIAM

no middle name SHAKESPEARE, associate professor of
English Literature at Peoria University where he also is
faculty advisor to the women's Glee, was born at Froud's
Corners, Illinois 61604, not really very far from his office,
Room #1564 Office Cluster, where he may be found every
single day of the week, hours: MWF, 2-4; TT, 9-10; SS, 1-6.
PROFESSOR SHAKESPEARE shot, according to the local
newspaper of the time of his youth (a weekly paper serving
not only Froud's Corners, but also Hinckly, Sweet Avon,
Marmouth, and Burth, and titled THE HINCKLY AS-
TONISHER) a dog in his youth. This death plagues his
memory and hardly a day passes but what he is accosted and
approached and accused, for it was a neighbor dog and
belonged to a boy with freckles and a whip. PROFESSOR
SHAKESPEARE, married, two children, denies he shot the
dog and is lately even denying Froud's Corners as his
birthplace. He has written many poems, some of which have
been published. His long poem "The Phoenix and the Turtle"

appeared in the December 1948 issue of the PMLA (Vol. L, No. 3). Since then parts of his "Dark Lady" sonnet sequence have been published in various "little magazines" throughout the United States. Also, our PROFESSOR SHAKES-PEARE writes plays. His first play starts off this way:

Hung be the clouds with black.

I like that line very much. He has written a play called HAMLET and another one called HENRY IV, which is in two parts. The second part was played in Laguna Beach last year by the Perios Players. The Zip Code there is 09372. As well, he is now at work on a play I think he will call KING SMEAR, which is going to be about a greedy old man who wants to have his cake and eat it too.

The King has a lovely daughter named Ophelia. He wants to marry her and set up practice in Denver, Oklahoma. No, I mean there Colorado. Aside from his many publications, PROFESSOR SHAKESPEARE is also a noteworthy teacher. His class in "Emerson, Poe, and Milton" is a yearly good favorite with the English majors going through our Peoria University. He will be well liked for years. We like him and expect to rehire him. Mostly we are a corn products town, but we are also becoming the hog center, ever since Chicago burned. We make Hiram Walker whiskey here and also this is the home of the internationally famous Caterpillar Tractor Company, Inc. (President is Ludwig Bonhoffer, age 49). Another line that comes to mind by PROFESSOR SHAKES-PEARE is:

At my birth the fiery founts of
heaven shook,

The frame and huge foundation
of the earth
Shaked like a coward.

What I'm trying to do here is give you some sense of
PROFESSOR SHAKESPEARE'S life and work. His wife, a
blonde, is named Bonnie, his two children are named Russell
and Bux. His dog is named Bowser. I don't think he shot that
other dog (see above). He is a kind natural man and would
not shoot a dog. Also, we expect to rehire him for years to
come. We do have one difficulty with PROFESSOR
SHAKESPEARE however, one we are loath to mention and
finally only do so for clarity's sake. It is not an insurmount-
able difficulty and I want to be the first to say that he himself
has spent many hours these past two years at our Speech
Clinic right here in the Peoriarea working on the problem. In
a word, he lisps. Dean Hoople thinks we should let him go
because of his lisp, and indeed we may have to, but we do like
him very much and expect to rehire him. I want to be very
quick to point that out. He says, "Hello, I'm Pothether
Theayksthpeare." I find that morally offensive and I think he
should be fired summarily, shot like a rabid dog. My Zip is
61606. I have a wife and a dog. I like to listen to my FM radio
with my ear plug. Many is the happy night I have laid beside
Goneril (the name of my wife, SS #002-611-228) with that
plug in my ear listening to Brahms Operas. PROFESSOR
SHAKESPEARE shot that dog, for sure. I also write. I write
poems. I wrote a sequence of sonnets published in the JEGP
(Vol. V, No. 4) entitled "The Loins of Francis Bacon." But,
PROFESSOR SHAKESPEARE has been working on his
lisp at the clinic. The best opinion so far would seem to
indicate that he is an incurable and ought to be tarred and
feathered and run out of town. I would do this myself except
that, as I say above here, I intend to rehire him. I don't have

children but if I did I'd name it, either girl or boy, Pontious. I like PROFESSOR SHAKESPEARE'S line about the "sullied flesh." Except of course his lisp wrecks it. Finally, I should say that we expect to rehire PROFESSOR SHAKESPEARE.

A FEW IMPORTANT WORDS
FROM BABY-DOLL IN GLORY

A FEW IMPORTANT WORDS
FROM BABY-DOLL IN GLORY

Back in those days when Peoria was known as *Dollartown* (or "Dullertun" or "Buck-City" or "Georgetown" (because the picture of our First President George Washington Himself is on the bill) or "Haul City" (from the expression *to get one's ashes hauled)* or "Ten-Penny" (?) or just plain "Pyourya" (as it was pronounced), back in those days it wasn't like today where anyone can have what they want long as they got the price. Back then, for example, there was no "messin between the races" as it was called. There was this heavy pressure on us girls from society back in those times to maintain the separation of the races, heavy stuff from the Mayor himself not to break the line. Times was lean then so this was pretty hard from an economics point of view, but the girls themselves pretty much upheld that standard even though, I guess it's in the nature of the trade, they were *curious,* if you know what I mean. It's just like any trade, you want to know the secrets of your competition. It's like that.

And so it got to be hard sometimes, hard to toe the mark. I mean imagine if you was a baker let's say and you got to go to Vienna only you was forbidden to taste or even look at them Viennese pasteries the Viennese are so famous for. You can imagine the pressure when you have all your professional instincts cut off like that. Well, naturally, we did what we could, since the demand was heavy. Let's say some buck come in of a Saturday with his wife and kids to get the week's groceries and he leaves them someplace for lunch while he comes to the alley for a little refreshment to his own liking. Let's say he'd like a little white meat to refresh his soul. One of the reasons I got my reputation as an artist so early on was because I invented ways before anyone else I know of to satisfy the imaginations of my customers. What I did then and for all my professional life was *Art*. That's how I understood it then and that's how I understand it now. (Except that now I make that word with a capital "A".)

So this buck would stroll down the alley and come around back like niggers is supposed to (probably better down there in earthbound if they still did) and come on in and one of my girls would say, "What's your pleasure, honey?" (I insisted on that.) And if the buck indicated white meat (or "turkey breasts" or "mashed potatoes" or "heavy cream" or "bottle of milk" or "Ivory soap" or "a slice of bread" and so on, you get the picture) this girl would bring him to me in my office where I'd prepare him, a lot like a nurse, let's say, prepares a pregnant woman for delivery. And we used the same word too, because it was accurate and kind of *professional* sounding, if you know what I mean. A girl would say, for example, "Don't bother Baby-Doll now, honey, she's prepping a buck." Don't that sound *official?* You bet it does!

So let's say this buck was a little nervous coming into my office like that, let's say he was a little high-strung, kinda *shaky* let's say, like a racehorse just before they shove him in the starting-gate (and also when the buck sees *me* maybe he thinks for a second the world was gone crazy and he was going to get him some *real* white meat. Maybe he thinks for just a second that *the law of the land* has been repealed. His thick lips part a bit as if he was to give out with "Oh Happy Day" or another one of *them* songs), so my first thing to do is to ease him off a bit by acting businesslike and official. "Honey," I'd say, "let's go sit down on that *white* davenport over there while our little Lilly (the girls for this act was always named Lilly) gets herself ready for you." So we'd sit down together and I'd ring a floor buzzer which meant the food was to be served, and then I'd begin the prep with the big *white leather* bound pillow book. I got that from the chinks or the japs, I never can tell them apart. Them yellow folk is way ahead of us, or way behind us, depending on your viewpoint. Anyway, I'd spread this book open using the buck's lap and mine and what I'd be doing was boiling up his water as we used to say back in those days and also trying to sell him the best act. It was like a menu, you could say. You know, where you say to the waitress, I'll have the #2 with white coffee. Yeah, I always did have a good head for business, even the Mayor Himself could say that about me.

Anyway, the book was art photographs, pictures of the acts done right here by my very own company, beautiful and exciting. I mean they was good enough to hang on a wall. So there was five "acts" in the pillow book and I'd begin with the top shelf as we say, with the $5.00 number, and I'd work my way slowly through each one. "Honey," I'd say, "just imagine yourself like this." And I'd be pointing to the male model. "Just imagine yourself, honey. How does that feel? Is that meat white or is it white?" (I got to tell you here that no matter what a buck paid for he always got the same job. That's an example of my business-sense as the Mayor would say. That way the customer feels he is getting something extra, something special, an extra helping you could say. Art and illusion is what the Mayor would say.) And so while the buck's pipe-pressure was rising, one of the girl's in a flowing white marriage dress with real Irish lace sewn all over it would come in with a little meal for the buck and the usual pot of Lapsang Souchong tea for me and she'd set it down and stand there smiling at the buck see and then she'd do something casual like rub one of her breasts or lick her lips. This would be one of my nigger girls, of course, but still it was, well, inspirational.

So I'd stop his attention at some tender scene in the pillow book, let's say it was a black kinky nigger-head resting beside a nice full milky white breast, something tender and motherly like that. "I bet you'd like to suck that, wouldn't you, honey," I'd say, and then I'd pour him a glass of *white* wine and cut a few pieces of white bread for a sandwich. After I got the mayonnaise spread on I'd say, "Now honey, which you want, some of this good dark meat here or some of this delicious white?" And I'd move the plate of cut meat over on top of the book in his lap. "Oh Mizz," he'd say, "de wh, wh, *whyte!*" The whites of his eyes bulging, his head sweaty, and his whole body beginning to stink like shines' does. So quick like I'd tear off a little piece and put it in his mouth all the while I'd say something like "Fine, ain't that fine. Here's I'll just tear off a little piece of this delicious white meat and you can have a taste." Then I'd leave his imagination to steep a bit while he chomped on the sandwich (niggers got no manners, you ever notice that? They always chomp chomp their food like pigs at a feeding trough, lips greasy and bits of chomped food dropping from their mouth) and I sipped the celebrated large leaf black tea with a distinct smoky or tarry flavour. You recognize that? You know, I memorized that from the teabox and I say it every time I drink that Lapsang Souchong. I say, "Now I'll just have a bit of this celebrated large leaf black tea with a distinct smoky or tarry flavour." So I'd sip my choice tea as we say and hit the floor buzzer again which meant that Lalita (I think of her because she was such a fine actress even back in those days and way ahead of her time) was to get into the make-up room where the boys would paint her and the buck would be chomping and gulping and peeking at the pillow book and that's when, usually, he'd come on the *chains* and point and mumble something with his mouth full and I'd say, "Oh honey, you like that?" And he'd shake his head off and I'd say, "But that's extra, honey. That's 50¢ extra."

Here I got to stop a bit and tell you something so you'll understand my Art and business-sense. At the back of the pillow book was these pictures I call *chains* which was pictures, say, of a white woman wrapped in heavy black chains on black sheets. She'd be in pain you could see and kneeling above her would be this black stud unlocking these chains and slamming it home while he worked. These pictures would be in a close sequence so that if you flipped them fast (just like the old comic books you remember) you could see it in motion: the woman writhing in pain and pleasure and the chains coming loose and the black cock stuffing the white meat. Talk about *acting!* Anyway, that was one set at the back of the pillow book. The other was a variation, only this time the nigger would be strapped to a pole and bound also in chains and locks and this delicious white bird of freedom would be unlocking the chains around his cock and sucking him off and trying to mount him and the nigger would be screaming something like "Free at last" his body bouncing in and out. It was these pictures what pretty much ended the prepping. Most any buck would ask for one or the other and come up somehow with the extra pennies. Sometime, and it didn't seem at all unnatural to me, but then I don't know of anything that does come to think of it, the buck would be weeping and gulping when he looked at them pictures. Like something broke in his nigger heart, like he was seeing his dear old black Mammy again after years away from home. It was pretty touching I can tell you. Tears is tears is what I say. That's what I call tenderness, and I don't see it much in the world anymore.

(You know, it may seem unusual to you to hear me say this, but you know I always did *draw the veil* as they used to say. What I mean is I make a distinction. I say it is logical that to build a fire you'll use some wood. I say it's logical for inspirational purposes to wear a few clothes. I say the smell of good food cooking is logical. I say it's logical to *point* at something, *toward* some object. Now, you see what I mean; where there's wood there's fire, as they say. What I'm pushing toward here is something I always insisted on at the White House (wch is #408 on the left as you go toward the riverfront, honey, ya can't miss it, all nice flatwhite and a model of itself in miniature on the front lawn), something I never permitted and I'll tell you I probably could have retired if I had. But come to think of it, artists never do retire. I mean you don't retire from the way you live. I mean you don't retire from the way you understand things in your life. Anyway, as I said, if you smell some good cooking from the kitchen it's pretty natural for your feet to take you toward that smell, eh? And it's pretty fair to assume that you'll ask for a taste, am I right? Is that logical? You bet it is, I'm talking sense. Likewise if you see some young thing all pretty in her shining shimmering pink flesh and let's say needle-point high heels which make her look all tottery and breakable and shaky and she's got herself covered with a thin string of cloth between her legs and maybe nothing but her hands covering her front, what this inspires in you is natural and logical and as God Himself would say, Orderly. That is, cowboys, you'd lasso that filly am I right? You'd rope that mule and wrassle her down and you'd put your brand on her, am I right? You see what I'm driving at here? I'm stumbling a bit here not because I don't know what I want to say but it's because, well, it's a criticism of human nature and that's not something I do easily. It's just that, well, it's so tearful, so sad and lonely. I guess I never did permit it for just personal reasons maybe. Maybe because it was so, well because it reminded me of my own pains maybe. It's like that line I was telling you about earlier, that separation between the races I was telling you about and how we maintained it at the White House. You know I am troubled to tell you this. Let me just quick say this. At China Doll's place (and I mean no disrespect to China Doll, I mean business is business and we maintained always cordial relations as they say) which was called the *Marble Palace,* at China Doll's place as I say, well, maybe it wouldn't be fair to China to say that. Let me ask you a question. I ask you, is it logical and human to see something and not want it, not want to have it? Is it logical to smell some fresh-baked pie and not want at least a taste, or a piece, or the whole thing with maybe some ice-cream melting into the hot crust? Do you understand what I'm talking about? Do you think I could trust you to understand what I'm saying, what I'm trying to express? It's one of those disorderly things that happens in human nature, it's almost a disease you could say, in fact if I was asked I'd probably say it was and is a disease. But there it was anyway on China-Doll's menu: column #1 was Orderly and column #2 was Disorderly. Do you think I can depend on you to know what I'm talking about? Like I say, I *draw the veil* on that kind of disaction. Partly it was to respect human privacy (and that includes niggers too), but mostly it was this other sad thing I just hated to see. So all that business went to the *Palace,* naturally. I'm not sure you know what I'm talking about. But I'll be damned if it just ain't too sad. I mean we all had our hearts broken early on and who wants to be reminded of that? At my *White House* we played it straight as they say. All thunder and friction, as the Mayor Himself would say God Bless His Memory.)

So there I'd be, the prepping pretty much done, the buck's waters nicely boiling, his pressure up, his armpits giving off that peculiar stink that niggerbodies always do, and so while our Lilly was getting set in the situation room (I would have sent in the act she was to perform on a piece of paper) I'd collect the fare as they say and write it down in my book. Then I'd give the buck a big hug and lead him toward the situation room holding on tight because I don't mind telling you sometimes my prep was so good they'd *faint* on me, *pass right out* on my rugs they would, or just start screaming them ignorant nigger words.

I'd open the door then and what he'd see! All kinds of things, just you imagine! And there would be Lilly as ordered, nicely powdered up and looking white as you please, white as an angel, as a dove as a flower as a cloud. Talk about Art! And so I'd close the door then, I'd *draw the veil.*

You know, I'm prejudiced just like any normal white person is, but I want to tell you something based on my experience. I think maybe you'll trust me because I tell you I'm white as you are and because like you I know there is one race and that all the others is inferior. So you can trust what I tell you and it may mean something to you also like it does to me. It's spiritual in a way, so since you're a Christian also you'll have some understanding of it. What I am going to say will conflict most likely with your understanding, but I've had all this special experience I think you'll agree and so I ask you to pay attention. I'll just set down the facts of this and let you see if they don't lead you to the same conclusion I come to. I'll try to speak as generally as I can so as not to offend anyone. As I say, I've got a lot of experience in a fairly narrow thing, I mean to say I've had a lot of experience with just a *part* of human nature if I could express it that way. The world speaks as if it knows about sex as relief if you know what I mean. The world sees sex as something it has to get rid of pretty regular, like shitting if you will permit me to express it that way. There is talk of "unloading" or of "getting one's rocks off" or of "getting one's ashes hauled" or of "getting one's nut" or of "tapping the keg" or of "topping off" and similar expressions. You understand me. Well what I want to say to you is that that is just a by-product and that something else larger and more spiritual is going on at the same time all the sex stuff if coming off. Let me be direct here because I got all the confidence in the world to say what I mean. What I mean is nobody fucks to fuck. I mean they may think and they may even say so, but it is the spirit, the devine spirit moving in them, moving *through* the juices they think they want to be rid of. I know maybe that conflicts some with your understanding of things, but I tell you when I mentioned this to God, I mean I just mentioned it casual-like, he said, "Of Course, Baby-Doll." Like I'd said something real obvious like if it rains you'll get wet.

It's spiritual is what I am saying. I mean you take that buck. In fact, you take any of us. Reunion is the word. That's what's going on, that's what. (Of course some of us gets more reunions than others of us. Some bushes got lots of birds in them. And so on. But the sun shines once a day only.) It's no joke. That's why, with all that training in Art and Diplomacy, I'm doing the same thing up here, on a different scale of course. There is the human heart in men and women and of all colors and it's weeping all the time. That's what I'm saying if my name isn't Baby-Doll.

THE OLD MAN

THE OLD MAN

In good weather the old man sits in the metal chair on the lawn. In his hand he holds a tightly rolled newspaper. He receives what occurs about him without response. If a passerby on the sidewalk ventures a hello, his voice croaks out a reply.

It is Sunday. Across the street, people are coming out of St. Patrick's. A woman is talking to the priest. She looks about. She is happy to be seen talking with Father Damian. He looks about. He is happy to be seen talking with Mrs. D'Aubigny. The old man slaps a fly on his arm with his newspaper.

A pigeon is fluttering about the slate steeple. Bells sound from the loudspeaker in the steeple.

Behind the old man is the house in which he rents a room on the ground floor. A window is cracked. Strips of yellow masking tape hold the pane in place.

I am looking for an old letter in a box under the kitchen sink. A starved cockroach flops onto the linoleum. The roach is dry paper. The roach scuttles off.

The old man is sitting on a bus bench with the fat lady. She also rents a room in his house. They are eating ice-cream from the Velvet Freeze. The ice-cream drips off the cone. There is ice-cream on her dress. She is smiling her idiot smile. A bus goes by.

The old man wears a grey felt hat.

Do you feel lonely, did someone leave you, did someone not listen?

Have you given up, do you devote your life to objects?

Perhaps you save stamps?

There are wild shores, my friend, peaceful places where the ocean smashes on the rocks, where the sea anemone is still surviving.

The fat idiot woman lifts her skirt. She is showing the old man her panties. Her mouth is rimmed with white cream. She says, "Peek-a-boo."

The old man has forgotten.

The old man kills a fly.

It is hot. The old man is stepping from the curb into the

street. In his hand, between his fingers, he is holding a strip of film, a piece of lead-in. He is wearing his winter coat, his grey felt hat.

In the shoe store the young salesman is fitting a shoe on a girl's foot. His wish is that all pretty women would come in to have him fit them for hip boots.

Do you have a dog? Do you have a cat? Do you have a parakeet?

A bus goes by.

Every woman is your daughter.

Who is paying for your happiness?

The church is empty now. Through the open doors the altar can be seen. A newsboy is sorting papers on the front steps.

By the window in the old man's room is a table. On the table is an old wooden radio. Also on the table is a roll of toilet paper. Also the lid of a peanut butter jar. In it a piece of soap. He is seated at the table. He is resting his head. One papery hand is touching the radio. He is wearing his grey felt hat.

Tobacco.

The dog is pissing on the rug.

I have red wine, some whiskey. I could get beer. Come over if you can.

JIRAC DISSLEROV   *851-904*

JIRAC DISSLEROV

#851

Sonya: "Fa! I may never get what I want, but I usually end up with something pretty good."

#852

Or did she say, "I never *know* what I want," etc.?

#853

Jirac is driving along the big American Interstate Highway like nothing he has ever seen with Sonya. Like most happy people, they can afford to be quiet, and so they watch as the scene rolls, cars, trucks, farms, fields, and repeats itself. Sonya says, "I wish I had some gum." A bus declaring: TEEN

THRUST FOR THE NATIONS on its side moves by. "What can that mean, Sonya, teen thrust?" Flat fields, a man standing on his tractor. Three horses grazing. A green sign: BRIMFIELD-KICKAPOO EXIT — 1½ MILES. A patch of blooming dogwood. Jirac takes the Exit. "Why are we getting off here?" asks Sonya. "You wanted gum." Back on the Interstate, both chewing good sweet cinnamon gum. Three flat-bed trucks carrying brightly painted racing cars. A license plate: MILK. "How about this, Sonya? How about 'Stopping For Gum On A Snowy Evening' as a poem title? What do you think?" Sonya continues her deliberate chewing. Three red barns in a row. A small plane up ahead, also following the road.

#854

"What ya doing this boring day. I'm so tired today and I don't know why. Kev I'm sorry for being so rude last night. But, Kev my only excuse is I'm afraid some thing might happen to me and then it will be hard explaining to mom. And Kev I don't want hurt anybody. When I get married I don't want anything wrong with me and people to talk about me. And hurt my mother. Kev, please understand I really do love you want to make love to you but, Kev I'm so afraid something will happen and then were done. You do understand don't you."

A note which J.D. found in a puddle on the sidewalk one rainy April afternoon.

#855

Telegram to the orphans: DEAR HAPPY WELCOME

TO ALL NEWLY ARRIVING ORPHANS OF ALL AGES
STOP GREETING TO THIS WIDE COUNTRY FROM
SONYA AND JIRAC ALSO ORPHANS FROM YUGO-
SLAVIA *STOP* SOME DAY WHEN YOUR HEART IS
BREAKING FOR THE PAIN OF MISSING YOUR
HOMEBIRTHLAND WE ASK YOU TO REMEMBER
THAT IN THIS STATES EVERYONE IS ORPHANS
STOP THIS BIG COUNTRY IS ONE ORPHANAGE
UNDER THE EYES OF GOD *STOP* EVERY ONE YOU
SEE HAD SOMETIMES HEARTBREAKING FOR THE
OLD COUNTRY OF BIRTH *STOP* ALSO THE ORIGI-
NAL PEOPLES HERE CARRY A BROKEN HEART
STOP THE INDIANS *STOP* BECAUSE WHEN SOME-
ONE CARRIES THE BROKEN HEART THEY MAKE
EVERYONE AROUND THEM ALSO HAVE HEART
BREAK *STOP* WELCOME TO THIS UNHAPPY LAND
STOP WE HOPE YOU WILL BE SAFE *STOP* THIS IS
OUR ADVICE *STOP*

SIGNED

#856

Sonya's horse is named: Venus

#857

Jirac is served a bowl of dry cereal. Waiting for the milk, he
is playing with the little bits, pushing them into little piles,
drawing his finger through. Above him Sonya is saying,
"Don't play with your food." As Jirac is saying, "I am feeling
my oats."

#858

Every living act is a re-en-act-ment, every act is ritual, is symbol. Value is the awareness of this fact; awareness that we are not alone, not new; awareness that each act is a piece of the ACT which is the condition of our existence. To the extent that one is aware of this, one senses one's life is valuable. For example, the dishes. I remind Sonya that washing the dishes is the central important ritual, that it is the act of renewal, that the plates and knives and forks and spoons and pots and pans rise from the foamy dishwater virgins, virgin plates, virgin spoons, and so on. That's what I tell Sonya, no matter what she may reply.

#859

Riding off on her horse Venus, Sonya calls back to Jirac, "Don't take a bath!"

#861

"This long act of survival." Lucien Stryk

Everyone is quite comfortable with the knowledge that this fellow Disslerov is a fool. Consequently, he is in great demand as a dinner guest. One evening our Disslerov was seated at the table of (   ) and (   ) in the town of (   ). Also at the table was a Japanese diplomat and a famous deep-sea diver. Happy fast talk all around, good-for-the-heart-company. The main dish is a handsome stew, Boeuf Bourguignon and Jirac digs in. In another dish is stewed tomatoes. Jirac puts two of these in his salad dish. Dishes are moving to his left. The Japanese diplomat and the deep-sea diver serve themselves in the manner of Disslerov before it is noted that the stewed tomatoes belong on top of the stew, and that the avocado and lettuce salad belong in the salad dish. They are many good giggles. Disslerov is shocked at how such a careless act can affect history. He does not think it is a laughing matter. Disslerov insists on the preservation of good manners and is dismayed when, by a thoughtless act of his own, the social survival of others has been endangered. That's what our Disslerov thinks. The stew is so good. Jirac eats many helpings. When it is time to rise his stomach revolts in a series of loud belches to the delight of the gathered company. Disslerov is embarrassed, near shock. The guests are laughing, offering milder burps of their own. The Host is giggling quietly, the Hostess is hugging Jirac happily. Such a good stew, such a fine evening. Everyone is surviving quite nicely, thank you.

#862 (for Evy & Morrie Warshawski)

They are all getting married, but they are getting married carefully, slowly, one part at a time. They begin with the floor underneath their feet, the proper place to begin any marriage. Next they marry their shoes. Do you, Pumps, take Loafer, for your lawful wedded? From there, the marriage goes up. The knees agree, 'til death. Then the midsections offer themselves in sickness and in health. It is going very well, this marriage. Very reasonable. Now everything is getting hitched except the heads. The heads are last, as befits this momentous occasion. The heads are waiting up above, directing this marriage of the lower parts, the necessary elements. Then they appear, the happy smiling heads, the groom, the bride, joyful attendants, all in their costumes. They agree to the proposal, they slip into each other, bravely, forever. Now they are all married. Very wise. We hear the showers of lucky rice grains pattering on the stone floor.

#863

Jirac and Sonya Disslerov biking through lilacs!

#864

Disslerov enters this huge sleeping woman on an inspection tour through her most accessible part, the ear. In his canoe, he paddles about her bloodstream. He is looking for information, he is looking for evidence. He is trying to find the answer to man's eternal problem: his fatal attraction to woman. He beaches his canoe at a breast and walks around. "There's nothing special here," he notes in his book. Little baskets of fat, an oily smell. Heading downstream, he hears what sound like voices chanting "mee — mee — mee." It must be, he records, the beat of the heart. Landing at the birth canal, surely a historical place, he finds only loose muscle tissue, hears a low growling sound: Disslerov calls this area "The Venus Fly-Trap" and notes: "Have pitched the pup-tent. Will spend the night. Tomorrow will do some white-water canoeing around the brain."

#865

Jirac is consoling his dog Charlie: "Cheer up, old fellow, it is man's duty to fail."

#866

These meaty, shiny, American women! These languorous loaves of lust! Disslerov is furious!

#867

Imagine what would happen if a woman dressed like that in Slovenia!

#868

It is spring again, ho hum. The women have planted their bodies in the ground, by bushes, along roadsides, in ditches, to gather in strokes of sunlight. They are waving at poor Jirac as he bikes around losing his direction. They are calling to him, "Hi there, Jirac!" "Hello there, Dr. Disslerov!" They are waving and that motion makes their naked bodies shimmer and wiggle. He pedals faster. He drives his bike into a brick wall, into a speeding car. He changes gears and drives his bike right off the cliff. At home, Sonya is planting sunflower seeds, baking a cake for Jirac's birthday, singing the old spring planting songs she learned in her father's fields.

#869

Disslerov notices that he seems to dream more in America. In fact, he says to himself, all the agents of evil are working harder here in the "states." He dreams of murder, of being murdered. Seeing women, his mind rips off their clothing. In fantasy he sees himself whipping six naked women tied to his sofa. There is a woman strapped to a pole beside his kitchen table. As he eats his plate of beans he tortures her while he carries on domestic conversation with Sonya. Clearly, this victimization is intentional. But whose interest does it serve? Do American men buy more Pepsi-Cola because of this? Does Pepsi-Cola relieve the pressure of these terrible fantasies? He discusses this with Sonya The Wise. "Why don't you," she says, "give them to me?"

#870

Jirac is having a birthday party for himself. Sonya hates the cake she made for the occasion and will not serve it. His friend Timmerman brings wine. His fellow Yugoslavian Taboric, a BUBBLE BEE. The cake looks like meat loaf. Sonya is unhappy, which is saying the least.

#871

Sonya is liking Jirac this morning. As he prepares to eat breakfast, Sonya says, "You know, in my dream house, Modest (she calls him that when she is especially liking him), we have two toilets side by side together so I can join your thoughts in the morning, right after breakfast." Jirac looks up from his plate of waffles.

#872

As he did back in the old country, Jirac attends the monthly meetings of the Peoria City Council with Sonya. It is, as he says, the duty of the citizens. On this Tuesday evening there is a group of very severe looking women sitting in the gallery. Their spokesman rises and demands that the City Council vote on a resolution in support of the Equal Rights Amendment, which is being considered by the Illinois Legislature in Springfield. This woman is wearing tall leather boots. She is demanding that the Council issue a statement of support for the amendment. Sonya stands up. Sonya is a big woman, not to be missed, even in a crowd. When the clerk passes the microphone to her, Sonya addresses herself to the question in this way, "Your Good Honor Doctor Mayor! I am Sonya Subasic Disslerov speaking to you. I am telling these woman to go home to the men and babies. I am telling these woman to not wear guns and boots. It is not biological. I am telling these woman to go make soup, to wash the floors and all the windows in the house. I am telling the men of these woman to do their duty. These woman need a good spanking. This is what I am saying." The woman in the leather boots climbs over some seats to attack Sonya, but a police guard prevents it. Sonya is escorted from the Council Chambers. As she walks past the group of outraged women, she commands, "Go sew buttons!"

#873

It is the middle of August, very hot weather. Jirac is looking at his skis. He is thinking today would be a very good day to wax his skis. Sonya asks him what he is going to do. He says, "I think I'll wax my skis."

#874

Women are the ornaments of the earth!

#878

The words come out of heaven from God. God directs them into the wombs of women where, like natural children, some grow, some choke, and some get ensnared. Therefore: God is the Word-Giver. Woman is the Word-Receiver. The task of the poet is to protect God and Woman. This is just a story, of course — what some might call a myth. But the truth it discovers for us is undeniable. If you understand this truth, you know why the huge granite statue of "The Sleeping God of Ljub" bears on His stone Body the initials of lovers for three centuries. This is also why the old peasant saying, "A woman's husband is her god," is no joke, no piece of ignorance. Think of it, just think of how many words you get from your wife. Just ask any woman. They usually know. Furthermore: given the light of this truth, we may understand that the Woman's Liberation Movement in the United States of America is the devil's plot. Also, we see that it must fail. The words come out of heaven from God. These words go into woman. It is not a matter of choice. The sun rises in the east. A woman is bound to accept the word of God. On behalf of God, Disslerov the protector asserts this. Also, Sonya Disslerov is in general agreement.

#899

There is a violent thunderstorm, moving up the river and breaking over Peoria, Illinois. It is ferocious. Trees break. A baby blackbird is thrown from its nest. Jack the cat rescues it and brings it in to Sonya, but it is too late. The electric power goes off. We sit in the dark. We hope the power stays off forever. Sonya begins to weep for the old country. She wants to go home. She wants to live in her father's huts, to pull some water from the well in the old bucket. A huge tree-limb cracks and falls on the front porch. The lights go on again.

#900

WONDERBUNS

#901

He's looking at women. He's thinking about integrity. He decides that is what women are for, or rather, what men and women are for: to maintain integrity. Without each other, there would be no integrity. From his position, women are absolutely essential. He is not quite sure, not convinced, that men are, that he is. Logic, however, tells him this must be so.

#902

Someone at work tells Disslerov that a woman can't think unless she has her make-up on.

#903

One thing this Jirac likes very much oh yes indeed is the whiskey, good Kentucky whiskey. It has a good taste. It is like drinking bread. He likes the color. He lifts the clear glassful to his eyes. "If," he tells Sonya, "there is truth in wine, then there is rebellion in whiskey." Sonya keeps her eyes on him, sipping her Pepsi with her eyes open.

#904

Oh Lord in this defeated time, in this time of moral decay, spiritual erosion, and physical exhaustion — oh Lord in this time allow us to preserve our illusions, our beloved dreams of peace, order, freedom, justice, and compassion.

THE TRIAL

THE TRIAL

A nineteen-year-old woman told a Circuit Court jury that George Washington, Jr., 44, had his hands around her neck, said he would kill her, forced her to submit to various sexual acts.

"I just got tired of letting people take advantage of me," said Bel. "It was in my home and I'm sick and tired of it." She continued, "I guess you could say it was the folks down at the Y helped me."

Washington is charged with rape, burglary, and deviate sexual assault. The woman told the jury she went to bed about 5 a.m. after writing a letter. She was wearing short, light underwear.

"Before I met those folk, I

145

never used my whole name. Bel, I was just Bel. It's what they called a *consciousness raising seminar*. It sounds dumb to you maybe, but they made me say my name. That's how far back I started."

I woke up and saw someone straddled over me. He had me by the throat and said, Don't move or I'll kill you.

"In fact, that's how we all started, just saying our names over and over to one another and we had this rule to always use our whole name everywhere. I mean like signing your name or answering a telephone. I know that sounds dumb to you. But I never said my name at all mostly, or just Bel. So when they said to say your name I said Bel."

The woman told the jury that she thought it was her boyfriend so she told him, You can stop playing around now.

"But they said no no, all your name so I said ok then Alberta and they said fine fine, that's a start, that's a beginning, a big inning Alberta. Then they passed out round mirrors to everyone. I know this sounds dumb to you, but I was sick and tired and these folks helped me."

She said she was forced into one of the sexual acts and the telephone started ringing. She said Washington had a shirt over his head and told her not to answer the phone so she told her cousin to do it.

"They said I had guts, I had the guts and I should use them. When they spoke to me they used my whole name."

He told me my boyfriend was with his wife and that was why he was with me. He put a pillow over my head but I grabbed it and threw it off.

"With the mirrors was another dumb thing I guess you could say. We was to look at our face in the mirror and watch our lips say our name. I didn't want to do it. I said I thought it was dumb. I said I could say my name a million times and they'd still come right in my place, my home."

Then he left the bedroom. I got up and looked out the window. I saw a white car driving away.

"But I was tired of letting people take advantage of me right in my home, so I went along with it. I took up the mirror and watched myself saying my name. I'd say Bel and then the leader would say Alberta, so I'd repeat that, just to please her I guess you could say. At first anyway. It was silly to see all those women looking in the mirror and saying their name."

She said she recognized the vehicle because she had been in the vehicle previously with Washington.

"It took me maybe a month so I could say my whole name without feeling foolish. It made me uncomfortable. I'd say it under my breath quick, or I'd mumble it. They corrected me. They said I couldn't go to the next step until I had done the first step."

She said she called a girlfriend to come stay with her until her boyfriend returned. Her foster mother told her to call the police. She said she didn't remember what she said when the officers arrived. Her boyfriend took her to the hospital.

"They said someday I'd have girls of my own and I'd have to teach them but I told them I already had kids so they said well then you better do it at home too."

The trial, being held in the courtroom of Judge Hentry Jackson, is scheduled to resume at 10:45 a.m. Tuesday.

"But where I live everone is hey, hey this and hey get out of that. I guess I don't think niggers is used to having names, just po black, hey boy. I know it sounds silly to begin with your name, with saying all your names, but you got to begin somewhere and it helps, I think it's going to help. I mean I wouldn't have complained about this unless I had this training here. I mean my case is no different than most of the young women I know. These men come through the door and they want something you got and they take it. I just got tired.

The complaining witness in the trial of George Washington, Jr., 44, admitted from the stand yesterday she had sexual relations with seven members of the FBI RANGERS one evening.

"So I'd say Bel and then I'd say Bel Smith then Alberta Smith, then I'd feel strange like everyone was looking at me and like you know when a white looks at you you feel like you done something wrong. You ever notice that, how blackfolk turn away they head or look down?"

Asked if she had reported the incident to the police, she answered no.

"But still I could feel those white faces staring and I mumbled until Beth-Bertha Mc-Nabb the leader said we was all in the same boat, all us womens was Hershey bars in the eyes of the law. She said, real loud, Ladies and   may I present Alberta Bel Smith. That was a signal which meant the rest of the class had to say my name. So that's how good Beth-Bertha McNabb is, she just got me through what I guess was my shyness. Why I be so ashamed to say my name?"

Washington is charged by the state with raping the nineteen-year-old woman and forc-ing her to submit to other sexual acts in her apartment. He is also charged with burglary.

"So then we'd all pick up the mirrors again and we'd say our names and watch our lips and if somebody missed — Beth -Bertha McNabb said if you ain't got a middle name honey make one up — we all start over again. And if you failed one of Beth-Bertha McNabb's *tests* you'd have to stay after class just like in school."

Under questioning by the Assistant State's Attorney, the alleged victim started her testimony. She told the jury of 10 men and two women she was taken to the hospital by her boyfriend Bobby Blue Browns about 6 a.m. the day of the incident.

"Beth-Bertha McNabb called me once to test me and I flunked because I answered yeah when I picked up the telephone. That's what I mean by a test."

She said she was pregnant at the time of the alleged attack and that besides her infant daughter she has a four-year-old daughter Jackwilline, by another man. She said she was never married to either man.

"I tried to defend myself I told her I never said my name because it might be some dude and I didn't want to be there maybe. But Beth-Bertha McNabb said bullshit I was to say my name and speak my own piece always."

The woman said she pleaded with Washington not to hurt her baby. She said she told him she was pregnant.

"They'd call up and say they wanted to use my place to wash their motorycles, I mean they'd *tell* me. If they wanted something else they'd come and take it. I don't think I see how that's going to change because I say all my names. I'm not going to tell that to Beth-Bertha McNabb."

She said the first time she saw the defendant
was at the South Side Social Club when she
was there with Browns. The next time was
when the defendant and four or five club
members stopped at her house to wash their
motorcycles.

"So they'd come in, maybe
one, or maybe more and see me and they'd say put yo baby
down moma and they'd be big if you know what I mean, a
black woman is nothing anyway."

She said she didn't know the defendant's
name, only that he was called "Fast Black."

"So I'd do what they made me
do to get rid of them so I'd have some peace onliest thing is I
never do. I got the strength to bring charges, I did that
anyway for now."

She told the jury of 10 men and two women
that she did not consent to any of the acts
which took place.

"I did lie to the jury partly. I
told them I didn't say yes to what he said I was to do. Would
they believe me if I said I would be cut or killed if I said no?
With all those men on the jury and white mostly? No black
woman ever says no."

She testifed she was writing a note to herself
about how Browns was going out on her and
leaving her alone about 5 a.m. on the day of
the incident.

"So Beth-Bertha McNabb has invited me to the *Poetry Society*. She says the old farts could use some young blood and black at that. No jive, she said. She said any woman who writes notes to herself is a seedling writer."

She testified she was awakened by someone straddled over her. He had something attached to his face and it fell off "a little bit."

"I write notes to myself, little notes early in the morning. I make up dreams."

She said she was never able to see his face, but she knew his shape, the tone of his voice, and what he said about her boyfriend.

"I'm tired of letting things pass over."

Previously, she said that Washington told her that Browns was having sexual relations with his wife and that was why he was in her apartment that morning.

"But I have to lie, it's my life we're talking about. I can see something is right but that don't mean I can do it. I raise the consciousness stuff, I just get up on that ladder and I fall off because I *live* on the bottom. Some folk have choices. There's only one tune on my jukebox."

She admitted she told police she was forced to comply with the wishes of several men.

"Maybe for my kids for the next generation coming on. But I want a little recreation too if you know what I mean. So if some dude takes me for a ride in his car I like that if you know what I mean. If all I can be is angry all the time who'd come by?

The defense attorney asked her, "Isn't it true you had sexual intercourse with seven members of the FBI Rangers gang in one night?"

"Some folks is so protected it makes them ignorant. It's like these club dudes. Suppose I don't satisfy them, what you think? They'll be on the women like that boy who popped that white in her backyard while she was gardening at her big house. She told the police he said he had to go out bust white balloon it was his initiation into the club. You see what I mean? These ladies got the idea they bodies is property with fences and gates. It's like that. They think you got to have *permission.*"

"Yes," she answered, "but it ain't no gang, it's a club, Judge." "The Judge is over there," said the defense attorney pointing to the bench of Judge Hentry Jackson.

"It's like the dude who raped those two schoolgirls last winter told the Judge. He killed them too and the Judge he asked the dude why and the dude said *because it is.* And that's they way I got to think. I could have a hundred names and say them all the time but if some dude walks in wants to practice on my melon I am not going to say no, because it is."

"And you never called the police?"

"No."

"But I got my own thoughts. I mean who going to stop me thinking my thoughts? You know it's like my foster mother, they'd be dudes doing her when I was a child in the next bed and she'd say well you done your damage for today. Then she'd get up and fix my breakfast and maybe she'd be singing a little song. I mean we got to live, like anyone else."

The woman said she made no outcry while the acts were in progress because she was afraid Washington would hurt her or her two cousins who were asleep in another room of the apartment.

"Beth-Bertha McNabb says I am supposed to tell myself I am a person in the mirror. I go along with the program but I am not no person just because I say so."

She said Washington grabbed her around the neck and told her he would kill her if she moved.

"I mean, if you make a move you could get yourself killed, fast."

The slender woman said she had been raped on other occasions and did not report the incidents to the police.

"I write up little travel notes like in the newspaper. My high school teacher always told me I was a natural writer for a colored she'd say. I plan these little trips places like Florida the white sandy beaches and Disneyworld where they have Mickey Mouse and Goofy and Tinker Bell walking around like anyone else. It don't hurt no one for me to write like that."

She said she was not harmed.

"Someday I'd like to waterski like on television, it's beautiful."

When asked by the assistant prosecutor why she reported Washington she said, It was in my home. I am sick and tired of letting things pass over and letting people take advantage of me."

"Far as I get is to the market or some dude drives me down to the Social Club or the Slipper Club. I mean I like to get out much as anyone."

A neighbor of the complaining witness said she went over to stay with her until her boyfriend came. "She was crying and upset."

"I was upset I had the baby in me I was afraid he would cut me it was hot and I was feeling crowded. I was just exhausted I mean I got no sleep since I was twelve. I'm exhausted all the time but I won't complain again. You know they are watching me I can tell. I can feel they eyes on me. But that night it was like the whole blackass world was sitting on me, right on my chest, you know that feeling? I won't do it again. Next time I'll keep it to myself like my foster mother done all those years."

The next state witness was the boyfriend, Bobby Blue Browns, 40, who said he lived with his mother. He said he was with a woman behind the Slipper Club about 4 a.m. that morning. He said he had a conversation with Washington about some ladies on a porch. He said Washington wanted to introduce him to the ladies but he refused.

"Or else ice-skate. You ever see the Escapades on teevee? They wear skirts and they glide around on that hard ice like they was in air. A woman has got to satisfy a man, how you going to get around that?"

He said he took the woman home about 4:30 a.m. and then drove to the victim's apartment. He said he sat outside in his car talking on his CB radio.

"Sometimes I go bike riding. Like with Bobby Blue or maybe Fast Black or some other dude. We ride up to the Interstate and let her out and the wind shoves my back into the sissy bar that's fine. Sometimes I put up my arms like a bird."

Then he said he went into the house and his friend told him what happened. Asked if she said who it was, Browns replied, "She said who she thought it was."

"I mean I need company much

like the next person. I live in this world."

Then the witness said, "After she told me all the stuff I went to his place and felt the muffler of his car. It was hot."

"But I got to give the Y credit, and to Beth-Bertha McNabb. It's good to have something *straight* in your head. I told Fast Black I'd try to make it up to him for that hassle at the Courthouse. I told Bobby Blue I'd try to make it up to him next time I saw him."

When asked why this testimony was at variance with what he told the officers at the time he said it was hard to remember all the details.

"Somebody said to me I didn't get justice from the Court but I say I did because otherwise I'd be dead."

The alleged victim's step-mother said the victim called her and told her what happened. She said she asked the victim who it was and she said she didn't know his real name but that he was called "Fast Black."

"This so-called consciousness raising is for other folk. I guess I got a right to live at least."

The trial is scheduled to resume at 9:45 a.m. tomorrow in the courtroom of Judge Hentry Jackson. The state is expected to rest its case.

"I told them they could wash their motorcycles over my house anytime they wanted."

George Washington, Jr., 44, testifed in Circuit Court that he was not in the apartment of the nineteen-year-old woman when she charges he raped her and forced her to take part in other sexual acts.

"You think they'd ever let me in the door of the Blue Shadow again? I mean suppose that jury found Fast Black guilty? Beth-Bertha McNabb says I'm only nineteen I got my whole life ahead of me. Sometime I'd like to meet Dick Van Dyke of tee vee. I'm thin but I got nice breasts. My step-mother can take the kids if I want to stay out."

The defendant, who said he lived with his mother, told the jury of 10 men and two women that at the time of the alleged attack he was recovering from an injury.

He said he injured his groin when a truck he was riding on bounced him and tossed him into the air.

"I'm just nineteen and I got a high-school diploma. English was my best subject said my teacher. I was in the Bluebird track in school. I have two daughters, Jackwilline and the baby I haven't decided a name. I like names with air, French names I guess you could say."

The defense called Dr. Richard Strout who

*examined Washington at the hospital and said
that he suffered inflammation and tenderness,
but it was possible he could have engaged
in sexual intercourse.*

"It was a mistake."

*The case is expected to go to the jury shortly
before noon today.*

"They look at me funny, like I
was marked."

*The defendant testified to his activities that
evening. He said he went to the South Side
Social Club about 2 a.m .and then he went to
his cousin's home and then to the Blue
Shadow tavern. Washington said he went to
the Slipper Club about 3:30 a.m. and stayed
till it closed and then he and a woman sat in
her automobile and played some tapes.*

"They told me down at the Y
this was America. I told them this is here. Maybe that's right
for them. Everytime I see that courthouse I think they'll
understand me, the judge will know me if I done right or
wrong. Those marble walls you just glide you hand along. I
read Jackie Kennedy got a marble house somewhere."

*About 4:30 a.m. they went to a private club.
He purchased a hot dog and some french fries
and then went to the home of his wife from
whom he was separated.*

"They can wash bikes over

here anytime and if they want something else they can take it. They don't forget I got a body. Maybe."

He said they ate the food and went to bed. He said the telephone rang at 8 a.m., it was a friend who wanted Washington to get him out of jail.

"I quit that group now cause Bobby Blue said they was trouble makers. So I go to the Society now, that's ok says Bobby Blue. His wife likes the little trips I write up. the assignment for next week is to bring in a dream. So there I am at Tup's Drive-In. I'm sitting with Fast Black in his big white car and I'm eating french fries and Fast Black is fixing with the tape. The fries look big and there I am squeezing ketchup onto them from one of those little plastic bags they give you. I'm milking that bag to get that ketchup out. The fries are good and salty, just the way I like them and maybe there isn't enough ketchup pretty funny ha?"

Similar testimony about the activities of the defendant was given by his mother, a cousin, and three other women. They all testified they saw him that evening until 4:30 a.m.

"Someday I'd like to get married. I'd like to get married like the pictures in the newspaper. Just to wear a gown you know I'd wear it all day and then you have those flowers to throw you just toss them out and somebody catches them."

Washington's estranged wife, Lemary, said it was about 5 a.m. when he pounded on the door to her apartment.

"Down at that same court-house, you could see the gown in the marble. Just get a blood test and go do it. All you got to have is $10.00 for the test and $5.00 for the license. And a little envelope for the Judge. So then I'd be Mrs. this or that, ha?

The complaining witness testified that she went to sleep about 4:30 a.m. and was awakened shortly thereafter by a man strad-dling her.

"What difference that make? None. I mean they going to leave you anyway, come and go an tip their friends you ready and so forth. But then you got kids and you be Mrs. this or that, some chump. They ask me hey baby what's yo name an I say hey dude what you got. You free they ask me, you free? They call me up anytime an there come a voice I don't even know *who* hey moma you free right now?"

She identified the defendant as her attacker.

"Sometimes I look at those little girls of mine and I see myself and like in a picture I see Moma looking down at me and she be smiling and handing me a little strawberry soda for a sip right out of her own bottle. I see pictures like that."

George Washington, Jr., 44, was acquitted yesterday by a Circuit Court jury of charges of rape, deviate sexual assault and burglary.

"It be something like 5 a.m. and they be pounding on the door hey moma you in there or knocking at the window hey sweet moma and I be saying I ain't free you wait and maybe the dude with me fraid he get cut and the kids is waking up and baby is crying in her crib they be hungry and the sun maybe shining in by the kitchen window."

The jury of 10 men and two women began its deliberations at 12:45 p.m. and arrived at its verdict at 5:45 p.m.

"Maybe they won't come by now, maybe they going to cut me a bit to teach me a lesson. They can wash they bikes anytime over here. If they ask my name what you think? Maybe I say something like pick a number. It's when the clubs get out, after 4 a.m. it gets hot."

Washington was charged by the state with entering the south side apartment of a nine-teen-year-old woman, raping her and forcing her to participate in other sexual activities.

"I got girl friends, but I am not friends with no black man. Because it is I guess. Boy friend is an expression, that's just an expression."

Washington denied the charges and testified he was with his estranged wife at her apart-ment at the time the woman said the acts occurred.

"I had another dream I was at this big lake or ocean I was eating a steak with lots of steak sauce mushrooms and onions all over. They was pretty boats

on the water all in colors like they was dressed up for a party.
I be digging into that steak."

*The trial was held in the courtroom of Judge
Hentry Jackson.*

          "It was in my home. I just got
sick and tired of letting things pass over and letting people
take advantage of me. I be marked now but maybe I can
make it up to them if they let me go. You be careful now, says
Moma an if you be free you let them know."

TH/ING

TH/ING

th/ing   42-2-6

(I will not have her agreeing to be my victim

Calphurnia awoke with this thing beside her face on the pillow. Touching it, she felt it growing out of her head . . . a thick floppy cock, a penis like a ponytail. What a classic, I thought, what a classic. I was delighted and jealous too. I mean I want to see a row of shark's teeth dripping blood, set in a cunt, one of those rare straight-haired jobs. Nevertheless, hope springs eternal in the human scalp . . . heh.

Well, to get it over with, I fell into the trap those two tiny noodle-cutters were preparing for me. Now when I was alone up there I was complete in my fantasy, they were my victims and I passed the time imagining how I would trap them and how they would do my didding, he he, and how I would work my will on their luscious bodies. I'd wake up, practice a bit, read a few scores, then I'd whip them with my belt before going off to teach. That's the kind of thing I did up there in Dr. Holes' apartment, that creep, that cockroach. Then I'd come home and have them rub me down with baby oil, then I'd fuck them until they screamed then we'd eat a fat bloody roast and they would lick me for dessert, right? Am I right? I mean I was intact, almost happy you could say . . . in the expectations I saw so clearly before me, or specifically, *underneath* me. Oh so lo mio, oh do re mi fa so la. Ah but I was a young man and therefore at the mercy of a force I didn't recognize. Gypsy and Maria, eh? You bet, but I ended up where I am now, a poor battered man, laid out on a slab at the county morgue. Love oh love oh deadly lu-uve.

(Peter Clothier's notion: *flack, flac* Flying through this flac, weaving about, maintaining altitude, zipping along over "enemy territory" on a bomb-run.

Making agreements with myself.

That Donna, that dumb Donna, just sitting there and *knowing* like that, me peeking at her bags, I means she *knows what I'm doing,* I mean she knows I'm gonna walk outta here with her right in LaVerne's face, she knows that and I'm gonna stab that Donna an she knows it, knows that too.

TH/ING   42-2-7-3

(or the Baron as villain-in white . . . the pure, driven man . . . humiliated by perfection)

202 allied chemicals

pork ribs, barbeque, red wine, a hard fuck "I blacked out/ I saw stars" morning moon in mist over messalonski (mama!)

Beyond Necessity

It's morning again in Sawdust City, Chipsville, also known locally as "Chicago" folks. The winter sun is shining in the chips, what's left of the birds that inhabit this place is singing off the top of her collective head, ka ka, there's no moon tonight the forest and rivers are bright cold, oh darling, slip me the seed of love. The lucky citizens also hark! awaketh! Another day hath come to Chipsville, another day over the footbridge at Big Titty, another day for the river carry the dead away. Senior Chicagoess 707 is already down in the bilges of Pussy, the river barge. Pussy leaks a lot, needs regular pumping out . . . otherwise. 707 is manning the bilge pump, in a manner of speaking. She keeps the rhythm the old way like choppin cotton and pullin corn in the ol southwest 'ho bam catch-ratchit" style. She's doin the "suck-a/fucka." However, 707 also hath a mind and heart, as do most folks, no matter how much they ignore that pump. 707 is thinking about the show, she's brought to town the famous kabuki story teller Bozo George to perform "Hamlet" in the glue factory shipping room. That's what she's thinking about, she's seen a lot of posters of that Bozo, that George, screamin his fuckin head off as Hamlet, gettin dead n all, and she's, well, inspiring herself down there suck-a/fucka in the barge bilge.
(The bus is ripping along, whipping north on the Interstate, it's the same morning as above only nobody aboard d'bus knows it's day yet, since they got the curtains down, no one

that is except the driver Peter The Great up front, he always
is, and in the back the troupe leader Bozo Geo himself who
has awoken restless and is laying the troupe Virgin on the
back seat to calm himself down. While he pumps away he's
got his mouth tight on hers, blowing into her lungs, so she
won't scream and wake up the other virgins in the troupe who
might also want a piece of the action. The seat they is fucking
on is over the diesel engine so it's warm and thumpy, an
inspiring spot. Feeling better after having done his damage
for the day, he says to Virgin 44, "You'll get a car and a boat
and a freezer and a quickoven and twenty-four cases of cat
food and a dozen menstrual belts, and a boat with twin
outboards and a pocket telescope and a mercury mirror . . . "
And so on, the girls love it, love to hear about something
specific like that they have won for being Layer of the Day.
They could listen to Bozo forever, he talk so sweet. " . . . and
forty range-fed steer, and a gallon of gas, and some
Covercunt eye shadow and a dozen fertile eggs, and ten
pounds of

th/ING   42-2-8-2

be ma li'tle good luck charm

    I remind myself there is a moon
    besame! besame mucho!

                semper idem walked down
                town to buy what had been on
                his mind since noon and his
                wife's denial of him. oh shit

James Mechem

were they lonely, I mean have
you ever seen that painting of
the two naked bodies, his and
hers, in that room? Oh suck
my stomach it was a lonely
picture, I mean it said we have
fed ourselves, and fucked
ourselves, we've gone to see
the moon, we've fished all the
waters, and we've just ended
here sitting on the bed's edge, I
mean they look so *reduced,*
y'know? that's the way semper
was with his wife now, so her
denying him his scoop of
chocolate whip after their
soup and crackers just hung it
in his mind. he could have
served himself after lunch, but
that was what she did, serve,
after all, and to intrude on her
operation would incite another of those tender catas-
trophes they had both learned
to eschew in favor of domestic
tranquility, and do I ever
mean it was tranquil, oh it was
placid, the quality of their life,
I mean it *hummed.* and so
idem was walking downtown
toward the Ice Creame Shoppe
with a scoop of chocolate
fixed in his head firmly when
he heard one man say to

another, "Well, thankya Henry, it was good working with
ya and besides we made a little
money too." somehow, that all
but knocked idem into the
gutter, those words made him
feel wretched, I mean they
were words of interest and
friendship, work and pleasure.
and measured by the ex-
perience of those men he was
humiliated to be walking out
to buy a scoop of choco-
late, the little treat that doris
had so carelessly denied him.
when he reached the Shoppe
there was a line at the counter,
a group of school kids, and it
was slow moving because the
ice cream was very hard that
day and the girl's scoop was
dull. tapping the shoulder of
the girl in front of him, idem
smiled secretively and said,
"I've got an autograph from
Mr. Elvis Presley in my
wallet." oh shit you know
what that kid did, I mean she
made idem feel like he had
drooled on his tie, pissed on
his foot, just plain *exposed*
himself y'know. Then he said,
"I think I'll get vanilla." Which
doesn't seem to change the

course of world events much,
eh citizens, but for idem it was
the beginning of what he was
later to call THE TROUBLE.

TH/ing   42-2-7

something in the way she moves
the one-a-day girl, she's sure she
gets hers every day
                    "according to mighty workings"
Calphurnia reading from the TV GUIDE

Senior Chicagoess 707 is walking over the footbridge to
inspect progress on her latest project. She's thinking she'd like
it to be ready by tonight, for Bozo George's appearance as
kabuki "Hamlet" at the factory shipping room. Imagine, she's
thinking, as she watches the heavy waters swirling and
stinking under her, our own glue factory, imagine the walls
resounding to the noble words of the Prince! Looking down
through the boards on the footbridge she reacts to a squadron
of pigeons flying by underneath. It unbalances her, causes her
to hold the wire-rope railing for support. She has seen his
picture, wonders how a man so round, a fellow so fat, can
play the play, can create the Dane whose part she understands as "thin," as "skeletal" even.

(frog legs and a dozen Italian sandals and a year's supply of
pie-filling for your freezer and 20 hit records and a date with
Roy Orbison who'll sing "Pretty Woman" to you all night on
his voice, and a weekend in Hawaii with the sex-object of
your choice, and a genuine Persian Marriage Mirror and . . . "
The troupe Virgin interrupted Bozo: "Hey, Bozo, what that
Marriage Mirror, what that?" "My dear, little ball of grease,

tenderfoot, that's the first way you'll see your new hubby, reflected in that cute little hand-painted mirror, and since you'll also be seeing yourself seeing him, your little birdheart will be gratified, for a man is but a pale reflection of yourself, a mortal man, a hubby, a cloudy illusion in your otherwise bright dreams." She looked at him directly, decided she'd better pretend to understand. "Yeah, yeah, well Bozo hon, go on with the list, ah?" "OK I can I do . . . enough soap to bathe the Italian Air Force for a year, a Gibson guitar with steel strings, a genuine imported French bidet, twenty-nine palms, thirty

707 makes it across the river. She enters the factory and heads into the cellar toward the mailing room where it is being assembled, where she hopes she will find it near completion.

Gretal/Glück

"I'm a (   ), that's why I've been picked
"I'm a (   ), that's why they picked me to talk
to you."

snapping forkfuls of mashed potato at each other
                        I'm ah well, human too y'know
                        I mean I have a thought once
                        in a while, like evry one does,
                        and it usually get me into
                        the same kind of trouble as
                        anyone who thinks, and if you

Ø

She is lying by the fireplace propped on a cushion, reading. From another room I watch her, the raggy dog asleep beside her legs. Outside the window, sparrows are messing in the bird-feeder. Outside it is raining, leaves floating down. Outside there are people under black umbrellas moving along through a sea of leaves. I am going into the kitchen to make some coffee for her.

When the Prime Minister heard the results of the election, he went before the television cameras and said to the people, "Whether or not it is clear to you, no doubt the universe is unfolding as it should."

I will not go back with you. I ask that you stay here, present with me. I ask that you resist history, whatever you are I am is here with us now not as words, more present than memory. I am not the mere agent of my past, nor are you. Hold me.

They are lying in their cribs, the little ones, waiting. They do not have enough brain to eat, or to move their bodies much, unaided. Their eyes are large and shining, their lips bright red, pulsing, trying to form at least sounds, give some shape to the noises rising inside them.

Unless you are here, unless there is some possibility of touching you, I am shaking, fevered, breathless. I am saying this to myself, safely, since you are not here. Now, it would be careless of me to tell you this.

BAZOOKA JOE and his gang bubble gum
FORTUNE: BE WATCHFUL AND
ATTENTIVE TO YOUR
INTERESTS

Why should it be you to brush the tiredness from your face?

Nahm, Namn, when I was there, what I saw, what I did, ceaseless in my head, I stay close now with my buddies and when we meet we drink and dance, our women watching us, wanting us to hold them, dance with them, but we dance alone, drunk, the music hard and loud, dance and think of going back somehow, to get back there where it happened, big holes in us, a sickness in the gut unless we could return, more drinking and graceless dancing trying to shake it off, at least go black until tomorrow, what I did, what I saw.

I will never ask you to trust me.

Today again, happily here, peaceful and glad, the cracked bone in your shoulder says it will snow, my broken toe makes no forecast. Thank you for lunch, thanks for doing the dishes, thanks for the coffee, thanks for letting me use your toilet, thanks for flushing, oh thanks for you.

We were bored, we felt useless, without hope, working only to make a paycheck, watching the second hand on the clock, waiting for the shift to be over, get away from the moaning of the children, hating their helplessness which was our own as well, so much need in their little bodies so twisted and starved, so much anger in us, tears, anger, resignation, their teeth twisted in their sockets, this concentration camp of the crippled, damaged ones, already dead, their eyes watching us even late at night as we pass through the wards, and we unable to look at them, keep on walking, do the job and do not see.

Lisa in her crib. Unable to move. Her eyes forced to look in whatever direction she is placed. Her bones warping as she grows. Unable to swallow, I insert the needle in her arm and food bubbles in the bottle as it moves into her body.

Keep them alive. Make them all live. No matter how, hide them away so that we may not see them, know them. Do it and do not tell us.

Rousseau: Now my dear, try counting to ten
His wife: One two threefive two one tentiten
Rousseau: You are dumb, you are stupid, but, I forgive you!
His wife: Oh, merci, merci
Rousseau: Now we'll have a quiz, we'll do the months
His wife: Oh, je t'aime the months!
Rousseau: What comes after June?
His wife: Jaa . . . JULY!
Rousseau: So good! And after December, what?
His wife: JULY

Rousseau: How can that be? I ask you, that July can follow
   two months?
   How can that be, I ask you?
His wife: Sait-on jamais.
Rousseau: How many toes do you have, stupid?
His wife: Sait-on jamais.
Rousseau: I don't care what one never knows, I'm asking
   you!
His wife: What did you ask, my dearest?
Rousseau: I asked what's for lunch, yes.
His wife: Sait-on jamais, perhaps a cheeseburger?
Rousseau: Bon.
His Wife: On a bun, you say, my sweetness?

I will now bite your ass.

I hover above you, bumbling.

As you pass by me, you pass through.

Oh, I was feeling old, was incapable, was in every
important way useless.

They punch the men, they drag them to their knees and
shoot them, sometimes the man to be shot is laughing as the
thick bullets smash his face, the killers are joyful, happy,
sometimes shooting their own bodies the men they are killing
are so close.

We make love over the wires, first thing in the morning.
Our voices entwine, holding and kissing. Your mother's a
giraffe, you're a wheat-sucker, I bet you don't know where
milk is from, let's ride the elevator all day, let's make a fire,
make love . . . at least, will you, have lunch with me, you obey

me, you meet me or else, I forget my name, my heart is milk.

You behind me, a strong woman. Behind you? A strong dog.

> *Rock on the mountain*
> *Fish in the sea*
> *A red-headed woman*
> *Made a wreck out of me*

Your asking if I want you makes me want you.

Your lips, your eyes, sometimes they are theirs, the little helpless ones, the eyes and lips of hopeless crippled children.

We are in the crowd at the Roller Derby, the proletarian ballet. Joanie Weston is jamming the pack, breaking necks, kicking faces, gliding through and making a pirouette on the banked track. Ritual violence, chaos and grace, a delightful scramble of noise, bodies in motion. We are laughing, hugging, but around us only stunned, brutal faces screaming blood blood. They are seeing and they need to believe. This is the dance of their lives, what they know. One of the actors is dressed as a doctor to treat the bloodless wounds. But there is blood, the faces of the crowd crying blood. And there is no doctor for them and we are wrong to laugh. We leave with the crowd, their silence and anger continuing.

She holds me in the dark, asking, "Drar Flay staffmeopof omendan?" "Karr, karr," I say, "denen oman binden flun derm offum coppertum."

We were so bored, counting grains of rice, watching the second hand grind out the huge minutes over their cribs.

There was quickly an end to crying, quickly we resented the little ones, wanted not to feed them, turn their warped bodies, wanted them to die.

This constant, this habitual hanging around, waiting for myself to show up until you come and stop it.

"Dear Mrs. B.,
. . . Thought I would drop a few lines to see if you were mad at us or Sick. You probly have been too busy these days. or Maybe you wereafraid I would askit you to take me some where. 'Nope'. I do not want to go anywhere. Manis haveit went to work yet. It shouldn't be too long now before he goes back to work when the weather break. I still have the stuff here that belongs to you. Jeffery & the little kids ate your Santa Clause's. The kids made some Bird house's to take to School the 7th of April. Tery Bird house is a square house made from a Corn oil can. Mark is made from a old Coffee pot. Linda is made from a old Boot. Melody from a sewing barsket, Debbie is made from a old thermos Bottle. Everyone here is fine and ok. My niece that her mother died at Christmas time. Her and Her Husband & Father are coming down this summer sometime. We had to get a refridgertor Saturday. It is a use one. It is a General Eletric. We gave $20 for it. The draus turn out isoxt. The Kids and I go to Church here in Douglas every Sunday. Lary & Debbie and the Little Well's girl went to a Jewish Synogg. tonight. Mark have gotten 5 A in Music. Lary is going to St Louis on Easter Sun. The Coach is taken a bunch of Boys to see a double header ball game. one of our neighbor's is dying of Cancer. The Place where I alway Called you from he was in the hospital a while Back. Mr Claude Staggs is one. His Family have to stay up with him around the Clock. Jeffrey & Timmothy are the only ones who stay home and Main that doesn't goes to

Church. I take Gloria and the Bigger one's. The Seventh
grade are having a Bake Sale at School Saturday between 8
oclock. 9 oclock. I am making a Bunny Cake for Lary to take.
Well I better close now.

Sincley Yous . . .
F.

Hope to hear from you
. . . Soon.
Let me hear from you?"

Nahm, Nahm. We beat at his face until he talked. He told
us what province he was from, he told us how much rice his
battalion ate every day, he told us how many men he fought
with, what kind of weapons they carried, he told us he had a
young wife and a baby boy, he told us he would like Merican
cigarette. When he had finished half of it, the sergeant broke
his nose with the pistol grip of his .45. Another man grabbed
his neck and threw him out of the chopper's door which was
open. He fell through the air like a sky-diver. His name he
told us was Nho something, he did not scream. When he was
thrown out, I felt the chopper lift slightly in the air.

You are free, free, riding your horse over the plains, wildly
laughing as the horse skims over the prairie grasses.

Come again the day, you not here, not in my arms, your
hand not on my face, your voice telling me it is alright,
calming my frantic heart.

Lisa is watching whatever moves above her crib, the
moving shapes of nurses and attendants passing by, the
shifting air, recording the life moving above her eyes, her pink
lips open, pulsing.

The aviator of the year chuckles about being called a cold-blooded killer: "When I kill them that's a few more who won't kill us. Everyone we get by air is one we don't have to worry about on the ground . . . it's a very remote war, airwise. I have a great love for flying . . . in an air-fight all the time you've got to be looking around. It's very self-satisfying when you do something real well."

Flying backwards in the dark, separated from the rest of the crew.

> Roses are red and violets are blue
> Your hair is red and mine is grey

I want to suck your little toe.

Climbing out of his long-boat onto the dock our bed is a pirate with a coconut face, fancy lace frills on his sleeves. Beside him all tucked in bed is a huge tabby cat turning into a monkey. You are watching a cracked, smeared, filthy scuzzy window pane.

My thighs smeared with your bright fresh blood. I love you. The poem we did not read says that, the poem you gave me.

As I watched them so pained, so awkward in their cribs, their wretched helpless bodies, I began crying, grieved, insulted by the offense my tears would be to them, mere tears sputting from the eyes of a careless angry man. Now it is three months later. They are still there, splayed in their cribs, their eyes still shining, bright, expectant. And I am still here, not crying, not crying. For the rotten mean person you were last night, drunk and scared, I have come in from the snow to punish you with my stick, punish your fragile body as you lie among your stuffed animals, my hatred worked out inside you. I crawl into the vegetable bin, fall asleep.

After she left me she took up with him. He gave her a color television set. She gave him a fuck. He gave her ten free lessons with a psychiatrist. It was like a screen test. He introduced her to his wife, to his son. He said, Don't tell my wife, don't let my son fall in love with you. Then he took his wife to Tahiti for a week. Then she fucked his son. Then the psychiatrist said, Why don't you do your own dirty work? Then she called me to tell me.

THE MESSAGE

THE MESSAGE

It came over the lines, the voice bearing the message, and
into the Yellow Princess magnifier, while Perfecta was
broiling the piss out of my half of the lamb chop, "I'm leaving
you," she said, "I'm leaving this and I'm taking the dog,"
whose bitch name is Take, and who was hiding her face in her
paws and growling while I was getting the message. I had told
her, how many times had I made the remark?, that she need
not leave, that she was my only, as the song goes, poe-zesh-
shun, was my ha-pee-ness. But then, she was going away most
every evening about five, every 34th of the month. Missouri
was on the line, god love him, his quiet show-me voice, his I'd
rather-plow-than-eat (his talk is of the plow, for example, he
once said to me on the Yellow Princess, "I'm gonna clean
your plow, Frankie.") crop-talk, explaining to my ear that he
had finally decoded — ("I broke their plow, Frankie!") — the
messages of the FORCES OF THE NARR. God love him,
Missouri, is what I said, "God love you, Hamlet, you're no
fool." Flames and smoke were in the kitchen, Perfecta was

189

screaming and the dog was barkkkking, but the code letters as Missouri whispered them were: HCT. "It's burning up the, Frankie!, it's, Frankie!" I had to laugh, watching the two-bitch dancing around my lamb chop, it was like a photograph (after 30 years looking at the picture he painted, Gertrude said to Pablo, "You know, Pablo, I finally understand that painting, what you were painting there was a still life."), like a piece of frozen sculpture, a little moral triptych. Missouri plowed on, "Ah figure it to be a mix of HCT, maybe two-three pages H, some of C, T folding in all along, but I think no more than eight pages total." Ha ha, Perfecta is throwing a white powder on the flames, screeching "c+++sucker" the way the Preacher does at the coming of Advent. "Ah figure Heroin generally starts it off, then C++t, and Time is the variable, the fixative, the grommet." So we had it at last, the code of the FORCES OF THE NARR. "Eat yr chop, get off the f+++in phone." We had their whole theory, the very basis of their civilization and their code. "Eat!" I'd have to laugh some, to think about it, then explain it to Perfecta, maybe get Missouri and his bride to come over, help us through the rough parts. "Would you? Come later with Dublin, we'll smoke." He would. Oh my god was I happy. We had the code! Fly me to the moon! My half of the chop lay charred and dead on our finest china. Let me play among the stars! Perfecta had left the kitchen to do a few shots of herself in the hallway mirror. I was left to eat alone in the receding smoke. Let me know (we have it!) what life is like (ha ha) On Jupiter and Mars. I can tell you I was swooning.

Bitch Perfecta, hash-head, c++t, addicted to as many versions of herself as the mirror can compute, Perfecta and her bitch Take, chin whiskers & a tiny goatee about her c++t. "Seductive is how I look . . . you want to touch me, ah? Any c++ksuckin man would love a touch, ah, a feel?" I gobble my chop. "Problem is," I say to her, "you got no holes. What kind of fool am I? Living a life full of holes. Life is a hole, H is a hole, time is a hole." "Listen," she says, "you a++hole, I'm taking the dog, I'm going home to mother where there's air-conditioning and young Jewish lawyers and doctors and indian chiefs, ah?" She shoots another view, rubs up a nipple, sucks in her tinytummy. "Ah, men, they *want* me."

I finished my chop in the toilet, looking, why not? at myself, which isn't so bad from the neck up at least (the rest of me like a bruised pear), fine bones, a weak, will-less nose, desert head. How many times have I insisted she squeeze my face, get at those blackheads? Will she do it? She will not. Strange dear, but true dear. I'll get a new woman, an obedient c++t, ha ha. Hold me, squeeze me, never let me go.

She's got her arm tied off, doing up, poking about the tracks to get on line. "Stiff me, candy . . . ohhhmmmistah Jones."

My turn to do the dishes. We all make concessions, compromises. While total service from the female of the tribe is my total moral and ethical ideal, I have had to give a bit on the dishes. I am scrubbing the broiling pan, burned grease, baking soda, and looking out over the valley and into the sky. It occurs to me that the code we have broken has applications beyond mere knowledge. I think of the Ma principle in oriental art, the gap that somehow makes it all cohere. The sky is a gap, the river is a gap between, the drain in the sink. Why is man put on this earth if it is not to organize? Missouri, surely, will have thought of this. I didn't do my dishes last time so she stowed them in the freezer. You ever try to get frozen egg yoke off your china? What the f++k, I an American and a democrat, right? When I agree to the rules I keep the rules.

Vagina, we may say. We assume a polite company. Where would we be without respectability?

"Nnnnna, Jooooonzzz comin down, mistah white light . . .

Frankie honey, you love me anymore, you want me go way?"
She's off, the c++t is off to H. The time is time after time, I tell
myself that I'm. It's a gripping scene, Perfecta on the pillows,
naked, snacking on a bowl of cold pilaf, the dog Take licking
her c++t, Perfecta trying to get her nipple in her mouth.
"Bring me the hand-mirror, hon, ah?"

It's coming along nice nice nice. Come on over here,
Missouri, bring yr plow.

The Mound of Venus, we could say. Or the Diadem of
Womanhood. Yes, we could say that also in polite company.
Box we could not say, it having been defiled, but perhaps
cabinet, something like Crystal Cabinet, maybe.

Thirty years before we were all together again on the dirt
lot, shooting marbles. So greedy was I then for my handsome
shooters, those beauties, those marbles marbles. Fire in the
hole, war! Then before that we were all in the hole with
mother who ate a pickle for us, God. But these are lies,
conveniences, the electric can openers of life, which, no
matter our wishes in the matter, insists on itself, and itself
alone. But those shooters! Try to remember and follow! The
feel of the fingers in the cool earth, scooping out the marbles,
the leather bag you kept them in, the lucky feel in your pocket
as you walked along, eh?

The rose? The flower of womanhood? (Not thing, or thang,
no, not them.) The jewel of the something? The meeting of the
waters? A piece of the sky?

"Ah, Missouri! Dublin! She's leaving me again, gone up
the track already to the land of Nod. Oh how we danced on
the night we were wed!"

"Seems," says Dublin, "to me Perfecta is making a rational
move. Hostile forces abound, y'know, I mean breaking the
Code will unleash the dog armies of the Narr. You got wine in
that skin?"

Little Dublin takes the wine skin from the fireplace hook

and shoots it in her mouth. Missouri starting firing at the mobile hanging from the chandelier with the BB gun. "There were we," Missouri speaking, "outside Bloo Castle, the drawbridge up, the moat poison, spears and other engines of destruction seething in the hot walls. It was then I said to you, Frankie, as you swooned to the ground in fright, it was then I said there'd be a century in our lives when with the use of our minds alone we could win the Ever War, as it indeed seems we have now. Now we *know* the Code, the Theory of the Hole."

"Ayeeee! Come in here, it comin AT you . . . Frankie, get them . . . Dubbie you get down here with me, you get ON this train, Plowboy, get a hack of this." Perfecta hath removed her wig, insists we sign her head.

Riding down Horse Alley on the Mound of Venus (Basket of Fish? Pie at the Y? Nay to that, forsooth, what would the Pilgrim Forefathers say?), well, I'm tired of signing her scalp in red, she likes the tickle of that felt tip tho, I do admit it, but beyond even our own history, into the blank page of the future.

Hero Heroine Her Her Ero . . . wrong perceived. There a dark innerward heroine down there, doing an odd odyssey, a lyric shuffle about the tombs of the past, a bit of trip of the good ship hole (I defend her, Perfecta, I am her defender.)

Missouri, the subtle one, the master-head, king decipher, doing a bit of rifle-drill with the Daisey. Lef sholduh, hams! "You know, Frankie, we got to consider the history of the double-breasted suit along with the old circus joke and golf. Consider: World War II did in the double breast, right? Remember how you crooned at the Copa in '44, by the way, were you fronting for the Mob then?"

"Me? Nah, It's still the same old story, love and glory, you know, Mizz."

"I do believe. Anyway, consider, if you will, ahem, the Hole theory we have decoded, consider it in light of golf, especially the hole in one, every golfer's dream, eh? I mean what are they doing out there on the green with their metal sticks? Hardly a game, golf. Everygoodman attempting what? a hole in one, right? Then there is the circus joke . . . see Sadie climb the greasy pole, the higher she climbs the better you can see her hole don there Johhny, where's yr ticket? Correct? Do we need more fact, more data, raw score?"

Dublin had a good idea. In the kitchen she was telling me how to have and to hold the restless Perfecta. She was telling me to arrange a divorce of those features I detested. I wanted to hate her bald head, but I was bald too, I wanted to hate her truck mouth, I did hate her cooking, too many noodles, her cake always dry, & most her holes, her having no real woman holes, the only holes being the heroin holes in the arms, stomach, ass, legs, between the toes, the little piggies. "Dublin," I said, "I live with a balloon. There's so little left to be married to, and I want to stay married, I mean I got to be married, it makes me feel, well, normal, you know?" Dear Dubbie patted my shoulder and said, "Y'know, Frankie, y'make a lot of sense."

Missouri has the Playmate of the Month stapled to a box. Her. A Her. He's firing away. "Can't seem to hit her c++t."

We might, the air being clean, the company polite, try fig, or bewonderment, perhaps it, is that masculine or feminine? But it is characterless.

"Missouri, I getting tired, I losing my wit, how much I got to go on this, how keep it going, I think yr theory busting up on the daily grind."

"Ya got another few feet, perhaps two feet, or in time theory, perhaps ten minutes."

"Bring me more mirrors, bring me mirrors and your eyes all of you, come surround my couch of snows, let me flash myself in yr skulls, hold mirrors before me while I touch my perfect body and you stay out of my bowl and touch me with your minds, I am your little chocolate-covered Eskimo pie, your Hoodsie, your push-up, get the camera, I want shots of me feeling so beautiful, remember Doctor Do?, remember what he wanted after years of the practice, how he got clear, what was it?, you got it?, he wanted to see my c++t, to gaze into the h++e, the crystal diadem of womanhood, ah? Dubbie, Frankie, Mizz, how do I look to you, am I desirous, you want to touch me, you do, ah?"

These photographs we passed around at the home, who could believe we had been young, been beautiful, especially Perfecta, especially Perfecta sitting now in her diapers and crying about the glass in her food at the Narrenschiff Home for the Aged. It was there they forbid us to mention our theory, not a hole, they said, a resting place. I insisted on burial at sea. True, I built a crypt at Pleasant Valley for Perfecta, but the sea for me. See for me, the one who lives there, is what I said. She was once a true friend of mine.

It getting late, another luckless day, more disaster. There no chances left. We all lying about now, Mizz and Dubbie smoked, Perfecta weeping and hungry, me blowing f+++s from the charred chop. Ah, we lost some more, we all full of holes and that's the truff. There was no reason for this, we'd have to return to conventional weapons, real tears, babies burning in their little cribbies.

We all shot, gassed, lying about on the pillows as the late news gets told on the TV.

Perfecta is up. standing above us. "Ya wanna see my pee-pee, ah?"

LISTEN, PAL

LISTEN, PAL

She threw open her blouse and said: "Listen to my gears."
She threw open her blouse. "And these are my boobs," she said.
"You're going to love them verrry much."
"It's not that the universe is unfair. It's simply indifferent," she said, throwing open her blouse.
"What we would call cruel."
"You got gum?" she inquired.
"Listen, pal, she purred, "you wanna stroke my flaming skin?"

The girl is nine, perhaps ten. Thin as a garden rake, dirty blonde hair. In the black and white photograph her figure is obligingly still, smiling. About her waist is a strip of rawhide, the ends of which fall along her flank to the knee. In her left hand, held lightly, is a stick, her riding crop.

199

She threw open her blouse.

The girl is, clearly, both a horse and a rider. Later, we learn indeed that she is a stallion, the leader of a herd of girlhorses. Further, we learn of their wild home, the crag-surrounded mountain meadow behind the school, the piles of dirt and weed and rock trampled by their thundering hooves.

Listen to my flaming gears.

We see the herd at play, romping over the meadow, the piles of dirt, whooping hollering hooves, neighing, whinnying soprano voices, whipping their sides with sticks. Back and forth and around they weave, sometimes crashing into one another, sometimes falling.

She threw open her blouse.

On the highest peak the stallion-girl has stopped to watch the others flowing about her. Her stance is proud, still. The wind is shuffling through her mane as she turns toward the low building in the distance. She is watching the building.

And these are my boobs.

A man is seated behind a desk. He has a magazine in his lap. He is looking at one page of the magazine, absorbed. The lower left hand drawer of his desk is open. The top of the desk is orderly, an inkstand, a blotter, a black telephone with a series of buttons on its base. To his left a tiered IN and OUT basket. To his right, in a silver frame, a picture of three figures, a woman and two children, a boy and a girl. On the blotter is a long, thin, bronze knife, a letter-opener. In the room are several chairs, all green vinyl covered. Also, by the wall, a miniature sandbox, pure white sand and some earth-moving equipment.

You are going to love them . . .

The door to the office opens and a woman, a secretary, walks in. The man slips the magazine from his lap into the open drawer by his left knee. He pushes the drawer shut, asks the woman what she wants. She tells him there are many complaints about a group of girls playing in the yard. They are quite loud, distracting the other classes in session. The man thanks the secretary and she walks out.

. . . verrry much.

The stallion-girl is back with the herd, seated in a loose circle about one of the dirt-hills. It is a serious time. One of the herd, a mare, is pregnant, about to foal. They must find a grassy place where she can give birth, where she can feed and wait, protected. There is much horse-talk.

It's not that the universe is unfair.

The man is looking out the window, toward the piles of dirt. He adjusts his tie, tightens it about his neck. There are, he is thinking, two options. He can issue an order, or he can cause the hill to be leveled off and seeded. He turns to his desk, picks up the telephone, pushes one of the buttons at its base, speaks into the mouthpiece.

It's simply indifferent.

With their finger-hooves, the herd is gathering grasses in the yard, returning full-gallop to the place where, it has been decided, the mare will feed and foal. From a hill the stallion oversees this activity, but does not join in it herself.

She said, throwing open her blouse.

The man is seated at his desk again. He is balancing the letter-opener on his index finger. He is wishing he had a dart-board in the office. He gets up, goes to the sandbox, stares down into the sand. He takes a tractor in his hand, pushes it through the pure white sand.

What we would call cruel.

The mare is whinnying her gratitude, bedding down on the newly cut grasses, chomping on a handful. The herd is gathered about the mare, watching.

You got gum?

A man is walking toward the herd, an old man in work clothes. He is walking slowly, erect. When the herd notices him they scatter, the hooves pounding on the packed dirt.

Listen, pal . . .

The man is seated at his desk. On his lap is a magazine. He is looking at a picture on one page of the magazine. By his left knee, the lower drawer of his desk is open.

. . . you wanna stroke my flaming skin?

JIRAC DISSLEROV   905-955

JIRAC DISSLEROV

#905

Note on the status of American medical practice: Jirac goes to two specialists to discover the cause of the ringing in his ears. These doctors take tests: x-rays, blood, urine, hearing. They spend Jirac's money freely. The first doctor says, "Hmm, I just don't know, turn up your stereo." The second specialist says, "Hmm, I just don't know, turn up your stereo." On his way out of the office the chief nurse says, "Hmmm, I have this too! You know what I do? I turn up the stereo." When Jirac gets home he tells Sonya about the professional advice he has just received. "But," she asks, "what is the stereo?"

#907

The obedience of women is a lovely thing to behold. When

206

Sonya obeys Jirac, his heart fills with love for her. He tests
her from time to time. This morning they were out riding
their bikes. Suddenly, Jirac commanded, "Bike faster!" And
Sonya speeded up. That's an example of womanly obedience.
It fills the heart with pleasure and love. Obedience will be an
important theme in future literary works by this Disslerov.

#908

We talk with great confidence about "animal instinct."

#909

Sonya and Jirac are walking the dogs on leashes in the
front yard, Jack the cat trailing close behind. A bird is
spotted in the grass. Jack leaps after it. Sonya leaps after
Jack, Jirac watching, holding both dogs back. The bird, a
baby, attempts flight, skims 12 feet and lands near a row of
low bushes. Sonya tried to find the bird in the bushes, Jack is
wailing in her arms. Jirac is watching. Through a window we
hear snoring. Sonya drops Jack, turns out her palms as she
walks toward Jirac saying, "Well, that's nature." We walk
down to the back yard to see if the rabbit has eaten more of
our young tomato plants.

#910

We have noted mentioned one of the great Disslerovian
dilemmas, where is my television razor? Namely, how he gets
lost in this tongue, this American language. Today's sample:
Helping Sonya set the table for dinner, Jirac has opened the

silverware drawer. He is saying to Sonya in the other room, "Sonya! I am getting the furniture!" You see what Jirac means, of course? It's a strange country. But not exclusively a problem with D. I mean, they tell you to wash your teeth with chewing gums on the television, nicht wahr?

#911

To celebrate the birthday of Marshal Tito, Jirac hangs the Yugoslavian flag on the front porch. On a small flag of white sheeting, Sonya has painted the number "83" in red, white, and blue. Happy birthday dear Josip Broz! Also for the occasion, Jirac has purchased the flag of the United States. It also is displayed on the front porch. While eating Tito's cake after lunch, Jirac is reading to Sonya from a little brochure called "Flag Etiquette" which he found in the package containing the U.S.A. flag. "Listen, Sonya! 'The flag should be hoisted briskly and lowered ceremoniously. The flag may be displayed at night when it is desired to produce a patriotic effect.' Well, what do you think of that, Sonya?"

#913

To experience American customs, Jirac and Sonya eat in a public restaurant once a week. This morning they are preparing to order breakfast. Jirac points to an orange swirling liquid in a plastic bubble on the counter. He asks the waitress, "Is that orange juice?" The waitress says, "It's Donald Duck orange juice." Jirac looks at Sonya, Sonya looks at Jirac. "But however, hoe-ney (all waitresses in America are called ("honey") is that real orange juice?" "Yes sir," says the girl, "it's Donald Duck!" "Please thank you,

hoe-ney," says Jirac, "I am ordering one glass of this Donald
Duck." Turning to Sonya, Jirac asks who this Donald Duck
is. With the authority conferred upon her by many hours of
television viewing, Sonya says, "Donald Duck is the brother
of Mickey Mouse."

#915

Do you hear the blues drifting up from the valley? Do you
ever have a dark day? Does Disslerov ever have a dark day?
Has there been a day in your life when regret filled your heart,
when the muddy cloud slipped across the sun? When you saw
the birds but did not hear them sing? When you knew the
lovely shining world was out there but could not see it? What
do you think, did you respect yourself that day also?

#917

These American women are very inventive. The problem
for each woman is to find a man to support her, so that she
may walk around freely in society, saying "my husband"
whenever she cares to. Nudity and face paint are two ways
American women use to lure men. But Jirac has learned
another way from his friend Moulin at the Laboratory. This
girl named Gwendolyn. She took to standing on her head.
She has a poor face but a miracle body, says Moulin. So she
took to her head. At gatherings of her social class she would
stand on her head. Thus showing her sexual accompaniments
in an interesting, upside down way. As a result of this
possibility for men to engage in unembarrassed sexual
inspection, this Gwendolyn had many offers of marriage.

#918

Sonya is watching "Another World" on the television with Jirac. Vic is saying to Barbara, "It shouldn't end like this." As he speaks he places his hands on Barbara's shoulders. "Why does Vic do that, why does he put his hands up there, she must feel terrible?" Jirac agrees, nodding, a puff of pipe smoke just beginning its long journey to join the gases in the ionosphere. "He should be placing his hands on her breasts, between her legs, isn't that right, Modest?"

#919

By some mistake, Sonya has seen poem #918 on Jirac's stand-up writing table. When he comes home from the laboratory, Jirac sees Sonya possessed by high rage, waving poem #918 at him as he comes along the sidewalk. Also she is uttering an old Slovenian peasant curse, "   ." "I did not say that, Jirac Disslerov! I did not say 'between her legs'! That is an ugly expression! I said 'around her waist.' That is what I said, you Jirac Disslerov!" Jirac climbs the steps and embraces his beloved Sonya, red and lovely in her rage. "But," he says, "what did you mean, my little nest, just exactly what did you mean?"

#920

Disslerov is trying to call his friend Moulin. He dials the telephone, hears a busy signal, hangs up, hears the phone ringing, answers it but there is no one there. He does this three times. Sonya is giggling in the other room where she is combing Jack the cat. "What is wrong?" says Jirac, "What am I doing?" Sonya giggles; "You are dialing yourself, you fool."

#921

This foolish revival of "gebrauchliteratur" in Germany. We did that in the 30ies. It resulted in such poems as, "Don't forget to mail before 2 p.m." Or, "Eat the 7 basic foods each day." Ridiculous. Don't forget to wash your teeth. Eat an apple every day. Salute the flag. Faaa!

#944

"What is the life of a beautiful girl like?" This is the great noble central question asked by Molitor Mathis-Dragic. It's awful is what it is. It is stupendously boredom is what it is. Imagine the head that does not turn! Imagine the male who does not respond to the paints! I will tell you the story of Sophia The Body, as we called her in Lbj. She was beautiful, she still is beautiful, eine ewige Frau (did you know that German is the second language of Yugo.?). But let me tell you about the quality of her life! It was awful is what it is, awful! Can you imagine it? Can I imagine it? Of course I can! I was married with her for two years and three days. It was awful. First there was sitting in the mirror with the morning face to wipe off the night cream on the face. There was the minute inspection of the face to see what was wrong, what was imperfect. This was despair point #1 for the day. When Sophia realized how ugly she was, how deeply ugly she felt. It was awful. Then it was time to paint, which was painful, painful and tearful — an ugly experience my friends! As the paints built up on the face so did the confidence of Sophia build. Slowly, stroke by stroke. Then there was the time of gazing at the face. This process I have been describing lasted each morning three hours. Then was one hour at least dressing. Usually trying on all dresses and combinations. This is despair point #2. The daily final decision is the result of exhaustion. Then there is a piece of dry toast without butter and black coffee. This is despair point #3 because Sophia is hungry as horses but must not lose her figure as she would say. Then there is going into town to shopping. It is funny shopping. It is shopping for opinions. Does every living thing turn toward her? Do men stop, do women rage? Do the store front panes of glass reflect correctly? Is everything working? This is despair point #4. Now Sophia is exhausted, correct? Yes. She must run to the home to be rested. In bed she has bad dreams about worms popping out her cute little perfect nose. She eats a bowl of lettuce. She looks at her adoring husband and accuses him of whatever it is she is lacking, whatever goes wrong. How can anyone like me, she is saying. Now it is late afternoon and Jirac is having the friendly feeling which he would like to share with Sophia. Jirac is feeling, as he would say, normal. Sophia, however, is in a rage at a little bump on her chin which she has discovered. It is the source of her beauty problems. She must attend to it in the mirror. And Jirac may take his normal friendly feelings elsewhere for all she cares. The rest of the day until the time of the sleep is dispensed in this manner. Sophia is reading fashion magazines and movie magazines from America. She is comparing. Is she as beautiful as Raquel Welch Elizabeth Taylor? Now she is eating chocolates also. They are forbidden and they do guilt her. This is despair point #5 and is terror. Jirac is visiting a lady of the evening by this time. Sophia is holding a hand mirror as she is spread on the sofa. She is watching fingers place chocolates between her thickly painted lips. And you ask what the life of a beautiful girl is like!

#945

I have been asked just exactly why we gave our animals

American names. Jack The Cat Tookie The Dog Charlie The
Dog (and perhaps Jack's stray sweetheart in heat, as yet
unnamed). The answer is totally private. The world at large
will never know. Think of it! At secret! A secret right in the
very heart of this America which has no respect for privacy.
Why there is no fear, no fear at all. We do not need secret
electronic equipment in this America. If you want to know
some private thing, just ask! I would like to tell you though, I
have a yearning to free my heart from the burden of its
privacies. But if I answered this question, what will you ask
me next? About my "manners in bed" as the great U.S.A.
poet says? Eh? Do you see? Oh say can you see? Ha ha ha ha
ha. Eh?

#946

The "Christian Dog" theme, for example. Has it occurred
to you how accurate that is? The early Christians were so
called, correct? The reason is this. If by accident I step on the
paw of my dog, he thinks it is his fault and jumps in my lap to
lick me until I feel better. Thus, the first Christians were dogs,
no doubt about it. Then the expression deteriorated. However, it is accurate to say that all Christians should at least act
like dogs. And that is exactly what Mr. Jesus taught us.
Exactly. It is a lesson. This is a lesson from Dr. Jirac
Disslerov, Ph.D. What follows now is an annotated biblio-
graphic review of the dog theme in western Christian
literature. (Did you know, for example, that our beloved
Charlemagne was called "The Emperor Dog"?)

#947

Disslerov is not ready to make "literature" of this yet.

However he does set down the brute facts concerning his
upstairs neighbor MAGMA THE BRUTE WOMAN.
  1. "a luscious piece of French pastry"
  2. sleeps naked on the outside porch in the hot nights,
     mosquitoes and flies swarming about her sweating
     body
  3. long black individual hairs visible on the left
     exposed side of her left breast
  4. her circus of fleas
  5. Magma: "have a good ride?"
     Jirac: "too hot"
     Magma: "yeah I know it"
  6. the muscles in her stomach
  7. the white uniform she wears to work

#948

The girls have arrived! We use them for women.

#951

MAGMA THE BRUTE WOMAN eats pork livers raw.
She slops a pound onto a plate and eats them with her bare
fingers. She is laughing and talking. Her mouth is open as she
chomps on the slippery livers. Pieces of the meat drop from
her chops. She wipes her lips with the back of her right
forearm, which, by the way, is heavily haired. To see this
feeding terrifies us. We would like to be her neighbor, but we
are afraid she will bite us. While she is eating we notice that
the flowers on the table wilt and turn their faces from her.
Even they are terrified. I hope I am expressing this fear
correctly. You will understand if you have ever met a woman

like her. Raw pork livers! Curiously attractive in some primal
way.

#952

In the U.S.A. we have "the best-selling and most widely
read poet of all times . . . his books have sold nine million
copies in hard cover." Here is a piece of his words: "a
woman's hills/and openings", hmmm. Inspired by this great
million poet I have composed the following literary effort, in
imitation and admiration of the best seller.

> *Love Poetry To My Wife In*
> *The Mountains*
> Sonya! Jirac sees you in the
> mountains.
> On vacation with your mother.
> The railroad train of affection
> Is chugging up the 5% grade!
> The boilers are stoked up with
> desire.
> Higher and higher they climb
> Toward the lofty snowy peaks
> of
> Pleasure. Mighty is the labor.
> Long is the way. Ahead in the
> Dusk of the evening lies our
> Destination, the Cockchornic
> tunnel.
> Stoke the boilers fellows! Ahead
> Lies our destination! Imagine
> it!

These Balkan hills adorned with
Sleeping women and railroad
tunnels!

#953

There is in the U.S.A. a noble and enduring veneration of literary figures. For example our dear Friend Remley has a brick on his desk. This brick is from the swimming pool of Hemingway. We are speaking here of Ernest Hemingway the Great Hero Novelist of the 20th Century U.S.A. This brick is from his swimming pool at Key West, Florida, U.S.A. Remley is holding up the brick, he is describing it to Sonya and Jirac who are very impressed and thrilled to have such an intimate experience with a writer who would be otherwise remote. Remley is describing how his mother bought the brick and sent it in the mails. It required a lot of postage and it cost more than a Papal Brick does during a Holy Year. It is an amazing large yellow brick. Jirac asks if he might hold the brick itself. As he takes the brick from Remley's hand, dear Sonya draws her soft lips close and places a Holy Kiss on the Brick. "How I love this brick, this Great Hero Ernest Hemingway!" asserts our dear and beloved Sonya Disslerov.

#954

In this U.S.A. today there is a language problem that, if Disslerov may be permitted, is both severe and dangerous. For example, the phrase "deodorant system." Disslerov has discovered that this phrase means "soap." Jirac isolates the problem, the *abuse*. It is in the promiscuous application of the word "system." Thus, in the U.S.A. we hear, "shaving system" (=razor), "nutritional system" (=vitamins) and so on.

216

On the U.S.A. radio this morning Jirac has heard this one
particular soap described as "a unique deodorant system."
The danger is that the honest and ancient word "soap" is
being abased. The danger is that the word "soap" may be lost,
and with it a little piece of honesty. Imagine for example if
dear Sonya came into my study asking for her "deodorant
system"? "Jirac honey! Have you seen my deodorant system?"

#955

"355. WANTED TO RENT
Two White ladies want
furnished apartment.
3 or 4 room house.
Call 7am to 9pm,
673-1905."
PEORIA JOURNAL STAR, July 4, 1975

Poetry To Two White Ladies
Dear White Ladies wanting
A furnished apartment or
house with a white stove
And a white sink and a white
Toilet seat and a white door
And white windows and white
Grass and white air and white
Steps and white telephone and
White trees and white lights
And white traffic and white
Paper and white poems: Here
Is what you want, it follows
from this point —

FICTION COLLECTIVE

Books in Print